How Dare This Stranger Say
She Wasn't Qualified for the Job!

"According to Mr. Hammett, I am!" Tiana fired back hotly.

One brow rose, carrying with it a devilish light in his eyes. "Many people are hired for positions that they are not strictly qualified to hold," the man countered. "It happens all the time."

"Not to me, it doesn't!"

Peter Hammett sauntered into the office. "So, you two have met."

"We didn't actually introduce ourselves," Bayne laughingly interposed.

"In that case, let me put it right. Tiana Spencer, this is Bayne Dahlquist, the top man here."

She should have known. Every masculine inch of his being shouted the obvious. This infuriating man was the director of the *entire* advertising agency.

PAULA EDWARDS
grew up reading *everything*, but especially romantic fiction. It was her love for the genre that finally prompted her to write her first novel, *Bewitching Grace*.

Dear Reader:

Silhouette Romances is an exciting new publishing venture. We will be presenting the very finest writers of contemporary romantic fiction as well as outstanding new talent in this field. It is our hope that our stories, our heroes and our heroines will give you, the reader, all you want from romantic fiction.

Also, *you* play an important part in our future plans for Silhouette Romances. We welcome any suggestions or comments on our books and I invite you to write to us at the address below.

So, enjoy this book and all the wonderful romances from Silhouette. They're for *you!*

Karen Solem
Editor-in-Chief
Silhouette Books
P. O. Box 769
New York, N.Y. 10019

PAULA EDWARDS
Bewitching Grace

Silhouette Romance

Published by Silhouette Books New York

SILHOUETTE BOOKS, a Simon & Schuster Division of
GULF & WESTERN CORPORATION
1230 Avenue of the Americas, New York, N.Y. 10020

ISBN: 0-671-57023-4

First Silhouette printing August, 1980

10 9 8 7 6 5 4 3 2 1

Love brings bewitching grace . . .

Euripides

Chapter One

With a fierce concentration, Tiana Spencer carefully studied the precise lettering on the closed door of the office: PETER HAMMETT, DIRECTOR OF ART; she committed the words to memory. Shifting the cumbersome burden of the leather portfolio under her arm, she took one final breath, letting it hum into the fiber of her nervousness, before she knocked on the door.

Three weeks of job hunting on the streets of New York City had sent the undeniable reality of the working world crashing down around her. Ever since she could remember, Tiana wanted to be a commercial artist, and when a friend of one of her professors went to England, Tiana made arrangements to sublease his apartment in New York. It meant dropping out of college before the end of her second year and leaving home in Georgia, but she was determined to follow her dream. Now, at long last, she stood on the threshold of one of the largest, most prestigious advertising companies in the city, the famed Dahlquist Agency.

"Yes," a man's muffled baritone responded to her knock.

Resolutely, Tiana turned the knob and pushed open the door. Hastily, she scanned the room. A lone male occupant was seated at a desk with his back to a bright, broad window. His head was bowed over a large sheet of paper suspended between his outstretched hands. He did not glance up. She gingerly stepped into the room and allowed the door to swing shut behind her. Tiana cleared her throat, and when the man still made no move to recognize her presence, she queried softly, "Mr. Hammett?"

His eyes stayed stubbornly fastened to the document before him but he stingily spared her a "Yes?"

Moistening her lips, Tiana began her practiced recitation. "My name is Tiana Spencer and I would like to apply for a position as a staff artist. I have my resumé and examples of my work." She paused then and could not help wondering if the phantom behind the paper was actually listening. A heartbeat of silence followed her unhalting speech. Then the long fingers of the man bent the top portion of the paper towards his sweatered chest and she saw for the first time a pair of eyes as brown as her own. Hypnotized, Tiana continued to watch as the paper was lowered completely to the desk.

With the elimination of the thin barrier, she saw the mysterious man was not so forbidding, after all. He had a full growth of beard, neatly trimmed and the same exact wheat color as his modishly cut hair. A closer look told her that his eyes were a darkened brown, opaque; whereas her own had a lighter honeyed cast, almost like cinnamon stone.

"Sorry, . . ." His eyes left hers to travel speculatively across the features of her face. They did a quick up-down sweep over the slender length of her body before candidly returning to her face. It was a clinically detached gesture, routine yet unmistakably thorough. He rose from his chair and revealed a long, lean, rangy frame. With a cursory wave, he indicated she should take a chair near his desk. "Have a seat, please."

Swiftly, she obeyed, thankful that she was not being routinely dismissed. The voluminous carrying case was balanced across her lap. She sat very straight. An imperceptible toss of her head sent the ebony curtain of her hair rippling halfway down the length of her back. For the only time since her arrival, a tentative smile flicked across Tiana's features and turned the corners of her mobile mouth.

Peter Hammett returned her smile before sitting again. Leaning back into his chair, he rocked it on its swivel base. His fingers were pressed together in a steeple and once more alert eyes scrutinized her. "Suppose you tell me something about yourself, your experience, training, your background."

"I've had two years of Art in college. . . . Well, almost two years." She glanced down at her portfolio and then forced herself to meet his unrelenting gaze. "All my experience is confined to school projects. I've done artwork for the school newspaper and the yearbook."

"Hmmm." It was a noncommittal sound and gave away nothing. He extended an arm across the cluttered top of his desk and commanded with curt professionalism, "Let me have a look at what you've got."

Even though Tiana took it as an optimistic sign, she felt a feathery tickle of apprehension dance down her spine. She cautioned herself to control her inner anxiety, to calm the yearning in her veins. Time was growing short and she truly wanted a chance to break into this field. The finely drawn features of her face were set in a mask of tension mixed with expectancy as he rifled through the pages of her artwork and read the neatly typed resumé.

"To be perfectly frank, we do not have an opening for a staff artist," he stated bluntly with no attempt to cushion the announcement. He closed the cover of her work and passed it to her.

Her hopes plummeted. The air left her lungs in a steady silent stream and she could not speak. With deliberately lowered lashes, Tiana blindly reached for the leather case.

"And even if we did have an opening, your lack of an art degree or compensatory experience would weigh heavily against you."

It seemed to Tiana that his words were nails hammered into the coffin of her dream. This was not the first time she had been told so forthrightly about her chances of gaining a position in commercial art advertising. But each time the searing pain of disappointment was rekindled. As she lifted her eyes, Tiana began to thank him for seeing her in a well-practiced if somewhat mechanical manner.

However, he dismissed her reply with an abrupt chopping motion of his hand. "But there might be another possibility."

Her head inclined forward. Her eyes glistened, mirroring her inherent excitement. Peter Hammett had thrown her a slim lifeline but it was enough to pull her back to the land of hope. A chance—any chance—to work in an art department set her spirits soaring to new heights.

He smiled briefly, his eyes clocking her reaction. "What I have in mind is a job as my assistant. Although we don't have much demand for your style of art, you do have some talent. A job as my assistant could give you some practical experience and in time open other doors to you."

"Oh! Thank you! Thank you!" she blurted out, unable to stem the rising tide of her eagerness.

"I gather you are interested." Peter Hammett chuckled, a scintillating glint in his dark eyes.

She tried in vain to remove the full smile from her expressive lips. But it was an exercise in futility. "I am very interested. Please continue."

He relaxed, once again setting the chair to rocking, as he told her about the job. The salary, while not overly generous, would allow her financial independence. She would come directly under his supervision and the list of her duties sounded suspiciously like those of an errand girl. But it did not matter. Nothing mattered now except that she actually had been hired to work in an art department!

Wordlessly, she conveyed her receptive agreement and he explained, "It goes without saying, the more you learn, the more responsibility you can take, and the job itself is not without advantages. Aside from the obvious ones of insurance plans and retirement programs, our industry is riddled with perquisites found in few other fields. We receive invitations, tickets, and passes to virtually every function taking place in the city. And, as you know, New York is a very special, very sophisticated city. The breadth and depth of activities here almost staggers the imagination. Occasionally you might be asked to go to something as a representative of the company, but for the most part, the choice will be yours. Now I think I had better get you some employment forms to fill out." Peter Hammett pushed himself from his chair, his hands braced on the desk as he leaned forward. "Can you start work on Monday?"

"Yes!" She nodded vigorously. One rebellious strand of her black hair escaped to trail over her shoulder, framing her piquantly oval face.

"Good! Make yourself comfortable and I'll be right back." And then his lanky body disappeared through the doorway, leaving her alone with her thoughts.

She had been too intent on her interview to observe

her surroundings before now. Curiosity aroused, Tiana appraised the room, which appeared to be an informal combination of office and workroom, owing to the clamoring array of easels, file cabinets, storage shelves, and a bench table. Photographs and enlargements hung from the display strips along the full length of one wall. In addition, two bulletin boards were loosely laminated with sheaves of paper. Whatever Mr. Hammett's talents, organization was not one of them.

Picturing the future, when she could bring some sense of order to the untidy disorder, Tiana failed to hear the door open.

An unfamiliar masculine voice demanded with acrid harshness, "Where's Peter?"

Visibly startled, Tiana whirled around to face the source of the intrusive question. Her brown eyes widened as they flew upward to stare into the piercing green ones of a man who easily commanded the space of the open doorway. Unconsciously, her lips parted as she took in the appearance of the interloper. Tall, better than six feet, he had the taut, sinewy build of an endurance athlete. His impeccable vested grey suit did not in any way camouflage the air of raw, primordial bearing emanating from him. It radiated like a personal aura.

Crisp, auburn hair waved thickly; his slightly peaked eyebrows only minutely darker by comparison. A faded fingertip scar rose quizzically from the right one, causing it to rise ever-so in perpetual mockery. Or was it skepticism? His cheekbones were high and chiseled with bold strokes above a wide squared jawline. The salient Roman nose balanced his features with an aggressiveness that heightened the devastating power of crystalline green eyes. The parenthetical lines grooved on the sides of his mouth placed him in his mid-thirties, while his mouth, hard but with a certain curved sensuality, hinted at a cynical amusement.

With an unnerving jolt, Tiana realized his mouth was actually skewed in amusement! He had been observing her as she had so unabashedly studied him! Tiny flames of embarrassment licked at her reddening cheeks.

"I was looking for Peter," he reminded her with a complacent drawl. Then he found it necessary to add, "Peter . . . Peter Hammett. This is his office." Impatience and humor set the margins of his expression.

"Yes, yes, of course!" she got out hurriedly, acutely aware of his needling and of her momentary distraction. "He stepped out to get some papers. He'll be back shortly." The heated color stubbornly continued to burn brightly as she shifted her gaze from the flowing mockery of his. In every respect, the man was entirely too intimidating. Having dutifully answered his question, Tiana turned with undisguised dismissal. Her back was again to the door and, not incidentally, to the disturbing stranger.

She heard the distinct metallic click of the closing door with mixed relief. Tiana was glad he had left and she was no longer subject to his knowing scrutiny. But at the same time, she felt an unaccountable wariness, akin to the total stillness before a storm. Even after he was gone, Tiana was sure some intangible specter of him remained to haunt her peace of mind.

She chided herself. It was positively ridiculous for her to be so tense, so unsettled, now that she had finally gotten a job. Shutting her eyes she willed herself to breathe deeply in a regular and controlled fashion. Finally, after the muscles in her neck began to loosen their knots, she opened her eyes. Gradually the lids parted, and then with a fearful snapping as she realized she was not alone!

Standing indolently near the desk was the towering stranger, as mocking and disconcerting as he had been on first sight. He had not left after all! He watched her with an abstract interest as the shock registered and her spinal column stiffened. With an easy disregard for her reaction, he propped himself negligently against the side of the desk, one leg hitched free of the floor.

Tiana found the look in his eyes too insolent, much too assessing for comfort. With a defiant lift of her chin, she pointedly turned her line of vision, but when she could no longer keep it averted, it returned to him, lured by the driving magnetism of his presence. All the while she had tried so valiantly to ignore him, his intense gaze had remained warmly attached to her face. She wanted to turn away again, but found it an impossibility. Pinned hopelessly in his sight, she had become mesmerized by the glittering energy of those eyes. How long she was rendered helpless, she did not know, nor would she have cared if someone had reckoned the time for her.

When he did speak, the trance was broken. "I haven't seen you before, have I?" he asked.

"No." Tiana felt foolish, inadequate, as she tried to shun the mystical effect the man had upon her.

Without consideration for her possible discomfort, he continued to study her with a decided perception. "I didn't think so. There aren't many around with your look. How do you know Peter?"

Tiana skimmed the room in hazy bewilderment. "He . . . that is, he just hired me as his new assistant."

The stranger nearly choked on the laughter which sprang immediately and unchecked to his lips, lips that twisted derisively as they leveled out to say, "And what, pray tell, happened to the last assistant?"

Confusion was reflected in her large luminescent

eyés. Hurt clouded her vision as a frown creased her otherwise smooth forehead. Why had he laughed at her announcement? She could only let the seconds slip by in shredding silence, until pride alone forced her to attempt an answer. No easy task under his watchful eyes. "I don't know. Mr. Hammett just hired me and he didn't tell me."

His eyes narrowed as the faint amusement was wiped from his mouth. "You're serious! Peter has really hired you as his assistant. Looking at you, I thought . . . never mind what I thought. So, when do you start?"

"Monday." And she mutely gave thanks no more had been required of her. She was at a loss as to how this man could rob her of her meager store of confidence. He put her irrationally on the defensive when she had done nothing to warrant it.

"I suppose you knew Peter before he hired you?" His voice lifted in question.

Try as she might, Tiana could not ignore his meaningful inquiry. "No, I came to apply for a position as a staff artist and he hired me as his assistant instead." She noticed the way his mouth deepened in one corner and some perverse streak made her add, "Mr. Hammett thinks it is an excellent way for me to get experience in the field. After I gain some experience I will move up to being a staff artist." Silently she hoped the art director would forgive her the slight embellishment.

"Does he?" His eyebrows went up and so did the quivering corner of his mouth. "And what do you think about it?"

Heedless of any danger, Tiana launched into her answer. "I think he is absolutely right. All I need to do is acquire a little practical experience and I'll be on my way. I've always wanted to be a commercial artist. It may take a little longer than I had originally thought, but I will be one." Her eyes shone at the mere idea of a dream within reach.

His smile tightened. Then his eyes shuttered as he lowered them to the case she held on her lap. "Let me see your work."

Before she could prevent herself, she was passing him the leather case. Instantly she regretted the action, but it was too late. As his hand lifted the weight from her, Tiana noticed he wore a college ring but no wedding band, and immediately she regretted that irrelevant observation.

Curling her fingers pliantly into her soft palms when they would have snatched back her begrudged offering, Tiana formed an ineffectual fist. Unhappily, she was compelled to watch as he moved to the other side of the desk and sat down. She desperately wanted to drag her eyes from the sight of him paging through her creative efforts but they rigidly refused to obey. She was held an unwilling captive to him as surely as if iron rings had braceleted her.

A fleeting resentment flared within Tiana. She found it galling to remain quiet while he so nonchalantly looked over her credits. Why this should be so, Tiana was not quite sure. There was something she could not define about this man; something that strummed the bass chord of her emotion. Taunted by a mounting frustration, she clenched her hands into resistant balls, the joints shiny white.

When he finally closed the cover and placed the case on the desk, there was a splash of interest in the depths of his green eyes. "You aren't half bad, Tiana."

The totally natural way her name fit the line of his mouth caused Tiana to blink rapidly as she sought a reply. She wanted to be profuse in her thanks, even witty, but the words deserted her. Instead, she murmured, "Thank you."

"But your talent hardly qualifies you for a job as Peter's assistant." An insidious mockery echoed in his observation.

"According to Mr. Hammett, it does!" she fired back hotly, incensed by his jibe and unaccountably defensive.

One brow rose, carrying with it a deviling light in his eyes. "I've ruffled your feathers. You shouldn't be upset. Many people are hired for positions that they are not strictly qualified to hold. It happens all the time."

"Not to me, it doesn't!"

If her outburst surprised him he gave no sign as he commented evenly. "Naturally not, since your resumé indicates that this will be your first job. What makes you think that you are especially qualified to hold this job as Peter's assistant, any more than someone else?"

"I . . . I don't know." She glanced away from him, afraid of what she might see written in his gaze. "Maybe luck had something to do with why I was hired. He probably needed an assistant right away." Her eyes traveled uncertainly to her adversary.

To her everlasting chagrin, he laughed. She swallowed down the bubble of humiliation threatening to burst in her throat.

A flickering of his brow lifted the small scar. "Young lady, with your obvious charms you shouldn't have any trouble latching on to a husband. I assume you are a part of the eternal migratory quest of women who come to New York every year looking for permanent mates."

"You assume wrong!" Righteous indignation lent color to her cheeks. "I came to New York for the express purpose of becoming an artist. If I can make it here, I can make it anywhere in the world!" Her vision was lifted high, a banner to her belief.

"Well spoken, with all the naiveté of a young idealist," he countered. "Unfortunately, I venture to say, you would have more success at managing a husband than in building a career in one of the toughest, most competitive industries in the world."

"How can you even suggest such a thing?" Her voice churned in grinding anger.

"One has only to look into those wide dreamer's eyes of yours to know you are filled with impossible ideals. You cannot even begin to contemplate the sacrifices that are ahead if you follow your goal. Your idealism, your romanticism, is in your face, in your artwork, in everything about you. Can't you see, that to achieve a goal like yours in a place like New York will cost you everything you are or could be, if left on your own?"

His roughened, impassioned words were flint to the wheel of her pride and the friction sparked. "Which only goes to show how little you know about it. I've reached the first step and happily made the sacrifices to do it."

"Only just!" he qualified. "Given time, one by one, your ideals will be torn apart and laid bare on the altar of success."

Her voice scaled an octave. "You are a cynic!"

Joyless laughter greeted her accusation. "I prefer to think of myself as a realist. But let us not quibble over semantics. There is essentially no difference in my calling you a dreamer, an idealist, or a romantic. It all amounts to the same thing. You are on a fool's errand, Tiana Spencer, if you think you can come to a city like this and blithely climb the ladder of success without paying a dear price."

He did not in any way acknowledge the swift hissing of her indrawn breath as he continued with a ruthless bearing, "Every year, hundreds, no, make that thousands, of girls come here looking for coveted careers, and every year, reality cracks the fragile rose-colored glasses of all but a few, very few. Out of that handful of survivors, how many do you think escape with their innocent dreams intact?" He made a derisive sound. "None! My advice to you or any quixotic dreamer like you, would be to turn right around and go back to your hometown. At least there you have people who care about you, love you. You won't find that here."

She would have felt less anguish, less hurt, if he had struck her physically. "I'm sorry if I don't meet with your approval, but I have every intention of staying." Her voice skated on the thinnest ice.

"Despite my warning?"

"I didn't ask your opinion," she reminded him unnecessarily.

"Granted, but in good conscience, I couldn't let you trip merrily on your way without saying something about the hazards you're bound to meet. You look as if you could do with a little protecting." His eyes, so green, so clear, glinted warmly.

"Well, I don't need a protector! Not you, not anyone!" she said, fending off his remark.

"You would refuse protection without even considering the possible merit of it?" came his pointed inquiry.

"Yes! You made that statement without even knowing me."

One corner of his mouth kicked up in a lopsided grin. "I could take the time to know you, but it isn't necessary. It's sufficient that I know your type."

Tiana glared at him mutinously with eyes like ban coal in a paled face. "New York is no longer the mecca it was in the past. Times have changed, so have people. Now women who come here for careers are aware of the risks just as they are of the rewards. Your attitude, your warnings, are from the darkest age of male chauvinism." She prized the slight wince her statement caused him, satisfied she had made her point.

"Touché. I find it difficult to credit you as a true believer in what you say. But I am willing to give you all the time you need to play out your dreamer's scenario. But remember, I did warn you." His face was inscrutable, his eyes cleverly unreadable.

Somewhat mollified, Tiana returned, "There are remedies worse than the disease. I think your warning is more poisonous than the treachery you say lies beyond." She smiled then.

He threw back his head and laughed. "That bad, eh?" When his face had been seriously composed, he was a striking man, some would say handsome. But when he laughed, Tiana caught a tantalizing glimpse of flashing vibrancy that lifted him out of the realm of the ordinary into the kingdom of the sensually sublime.

It brought to the fore implications she could not even begin to fathom. A feeling of keen enjoyment welled within her and erupted from her lips in responsive laughter. The acid of their disagreement was dissolved in a moment of shared humor.

"I would give much to know what you two find so funny." Peter Hammett sauntered casually into the office. Carelessly, he dropped some papers on the crowded desk before pulling over a third chair.

Tiana's expression sobered as he sat down. The last vestige of shared humor was erased from her mouth.

Peter Hammett's eyes traveled pensively from Tiana to the other man and back to her. "So, you two have met. Good! After we got the paperwork squared away, I intended to take you by to meet Bayne." Then he glanced over to the other man, "By the way, did you want to see me about anything in particular?"

"It will keep." The man Bayne rejoined.

Tiana's worst fears were realized. It was more than apparent the one named Bayne was connected with the agency. Somehow, she had nourished the silly hope that he was passing through and not a part of the organization that now employed her.

The auburn-headed man shot her an oblique look before asking, "Since when were you in the market for an assistant, Peter?"

"Since about thirty minutes ago," Peter Hammett chuckled. "When Tiana walked in, I couldn't resist. Can you blame me?"

Bayne tossed a scoring look at Tiana, tallying a winning point in his favor. "You aren't saying you hired her for reasons other than her artistic flair?" he questioned with barely suppressible irony.

"Might have!" Peter laughed. "I followed a hunch. Seriously, some of her work is pretty good. Have you seen it?"

"I looked it over," he admitted. "Much to Tiana's distress."

Startled, Tiana jerked her head in his direction, literally daring him to continue in such a seditious track in front of her new boss. If she had been under any illusion that the path between them was smoothed, he had certainly disabused her of that fanciful notion.

"Did Bayne upset you, Tiana?" Peter Hammett asked, his brow ribbed with curiosity.

"Mr. Hammett, I—" She was at a loss on how to explain what Bayne did to her. She wasn't even sure herself!

"Peter." The art director corrected her. "Didn't Bayne tell you we are very informal here?"

Her eyes zipped from one man to the other, confounded by which question to answer. With a kind of awkward nod, she managed, "No, not exactly, Peter." She hoped it would have answered either question, both, or none at all. Sweet mercy, she was making a mess of it.

But further tangles were forestalled when Bayne laughingly interposed, "Tiana and I did not actually introduce ourselves."

Peter made a sound deep in his throat, a cartel of levity and expectation. "In that case, let me put it right. Tiana Spencer—Bayne Dahlquist, the top man here."

She should have known! She would have known! If only Bayne Dahlquist had not been so intimidating, so interfering, logic alone would have persuaded her to guess he was the director of the entire Dahlquist Agency. Every masculine inch of his being shouted the obvious. With a stiff movement of her head, she acknowledged, "Mr. Dahlquist."

"Bayne," he corrected. "Peter is right, we are informal here." A silent laughter rode his voice.

Tiana longed for the ability to ignore the softly spoken request. But even if she could have accomplished the impossibility of ignoring the man, she could never disregard the director of the agency who had employed her. She was graceful in her defeat, "Bayne."

Her reward was another dazzling smile, and like a mindless marionette, she smiled in return. All her negative feelings about the man were annulled with one spontaneous gesture.

True, Bayne Dahlquist had accused her of being a romantic idealist. And Tiana knew him to be a cynic, but together they did share an invisible shell of common humanity, delicate though it was. Would it be enough to overcome their differences? Or was her hope preordained to failure because Bayne thought her on a fool's errand, a quixotic quest? Mentally, Tiana up-braided herself for such an unfounded fear. She reminded herself that with the whole of the agency's heirarchy separating them, she was not likely to see much of Bayne Dahlquist. And for that small gift of the gods, Tiana would be eternally thankful!

Chapter Two

The battered yellow taxi was weaving its way through the midtown Manhattan traffic almost before Tiana had settled in the back seat. The towering walls of the skyscrapers loomed over the slashes of asphalt. And the lavender greying of the sky deepened to herald the approach of another early spring night as the hired car crept toward her apartment in the city's SoHo district.

As an artist's creative colony, SoHo lacked the intense tourist appeal of Greenwich Village but it proved to be an ideal place for living. Happily, Tiana found that it had a virtual cornucopia of neighborhood attractions; stores, shops, galleries, and restaurants dotted its picturesque streets. The name SoHo is an acronym of South Houston, one of the streets forming its boundary, and it was nicknamed the Cast Iron District in recognition of its many buildings constructed of that material. In fact, Tiana's apartment was located in one such building built in the mid 1880's.

In her unbridled elation over her new job, Tiana had decided to take a cab home instead of enduring the bruising hustle of the rush-hour subway. She had spent the greater part of the hectic afternoon at the Dahlquist Agency. As Peter had promised, there had been a stack of employment forms. But, after they had been successfully dealt with, he had thoughtfully shown her around the agency on what he jokingly referred to as the "grand tour." She had been mildly surprised to see how extensive the company was, occupying a full floor of the Madison Avenue building. There was a honeycomb of corridors connecting a mesh of inner offices and workrooms. Any doubt Tiana may have had about the friendliness of the staff vanished as she was introduced. To the last man and woman, her welcome had been extremely cordial.

After paying and tipping the driver, Tiana raced up the four flights of stairs to her flat. It had only one main room with neat alcoves budding into the kitchen and sleeping areas. She deposited her shoulder bag on an end table and let her portfolio slide to the floor to rest against the wall before double-bolting the door. She glanced over at the partially covered canvas on the easel across the room as she walked over to the telephone. With a wry grimace, she promised herself that she would fit her schedule with more time for painting. Now that she had a job, there would be no more excuses. Perhaps she would advance her training by taking a night class at one of the city's art centers.

Tiana telephoned the news about her job to her parents, who, if not wholeheartedly pleased, were at least interested in her progress. Initially, her father, a classics professor at a small private college in Georgia, had been most adamant in his opposition to her plan to drop out of school in order to move to New York. Her mother, on the other hand, had interceded in Tiana's behalf. It might have been because her mother had once wanted to be a professional dancer and had given up that hope when she married. Whatever the reason, Tiana was grateful when her father was persuaded to give her financial support while she looked for a job. But there had been one binding condition to the family arrangement. If Tiana did not find a self-supporting job within two months, she would return home and enroll in college for the summer session. Luckily, because of the job she had gotten as Peter's assistant, Tiana would not have to yield to her father's wish.

The obligatory call over, Tiana began a methodical pillaging of the cupboards serving as the storage section of her kitchen. As she grabbed a can of tuna fish, the phone rang. Thinking it was her parents with yet another concern, Tiana hastened to answer it with the small can still in her hand.

"Hello!" she chortled.

"Tiana? Peter Hammett," came the curt identification. "Do you have any plans tonight?"

She inspected the can with a jaundiced eye and laughingly retorted, "No, not really."

"I'm going to the gallery opening for Lewis Starke's major retrospective. How would you like to come along?"

"I'd love it!" She knew that Lewis Starke was well respected in the world of avant-garde art and invitations to the opening of his exhibition would be at a premium. "Are you sure it will be all right?"

"Absolutely! But there's one thing I want you to understand, Tiana. I'll be doing some work, so you will have to be on your own for a while."

"You'll be working?"

"Yes, I'll be taking some pictures for one of our local magazines. But it shouldn't interfere with you seeing the exhibit if you don't mind being on your own."

"No, I don't mind at all," she responded.

"Good! If you can make it by seven, we can have dinner first."

"Seven is perfect!" Tiana announced without thinking.

"I'll have the cab waiting so be ready when I ring," Peter forewarned.

"Would you rather I meet you?" she offered.

"No, just be dressed. By the way this thing is formal. Is that a problem?" he asked offhandedly.

"Not at all," she assured him before he hung up. With the limited time allotted to her by Peter, Tiana hurried her bath before donning a black floor-length gown. It was a classical shirtwaisted style with a matching sash that accented the slim girth of her waist. She slipped into a pair of patent leather high heel sandals before puzzling about the way to comb her hair. Deciding on a loose knot on top of her head, Tiana entwined all but a few strands, which she left to curl in whimsical tendrils against her cheeks. She applied the thinnest film of makeup before enveloping herself in a fragrant cologne.

Brilliant indirect lighting flooded the lobby of the gallery. A growing crowd of the city's beautiful people were already milling around when Tiana and Peter arrived. He took her hand in his and led her to an inconspicuous security stand where he showed the guard several cards and in return was issued a clearance pass for his camera. While the attendant wrote down some information, Tiana's gaze dodged throughout the assemblage. A momentary stabbing of discomfort arose as she noticed most of the women present were wearing luxurious furs and jewels, but the observation barely registered before Peter pocketed his pass and handed her an exhibition catalog.

Peter led her around the congestion in the outer lobby into the relatively deserted display room. However, they had scarcely viewed three of the works before he lowered his head to whisper in her ear,

"Listen, the others are starting to filter in now and I need to circulate. Will you be all right for a while?"

"Don't worry. You go ahead." She glanced up at him, catching a wag of his head before he was shouldering his way around a cluster of patrons. With a gentle sigh, Tiana watched him disappear through the flowing archway before turning her attention to the catalog.

The work of Lewis Starke was familiar to her through examples she had seen pictured in some of her art books. Although Tiana was not particularly fond of his kind of art, she admired the technical and creative execution of his skill. Common household and industrial objects were transformed into severe and often ironical distortions of their original forms.

Tiana was totally engrossed in one of the sculptures when a remembered voice breathed from behind her, "Don't tell me you are one of Starke's devotees?"

Startled by the resonantly unique sound of Bayne Dahlquist's voice, Tiana spun around. Her golden flecked brown eyes locked with his splintery green ones as her heart hammered violently. "Not really." Mindful of his unsettling proximity, Tiana ordered herself to take a step backward. Only then did she see the woman standing next to him.

A willowy redhead stood level with him. Simply stated, the woman was stunning. Although she was not actually smiling, a flickering light passed behind the most jewellike green eyes Tiana had ever encountered. The green eyes met and matched the fire in the emeralds in her necklace while their deepest hue was picked up and repeated in a gown of variegated shades of green. As the woman brought up a lovely manicured hand to rest on the sleeve of Bayne's tuxedo jacket, Tiana recognized her. She was the most widely photo-

graphed model in the world. Her face had adorned the
covers of more magazines than any other model in the
history of advertising.

At the model's touch, Bayne turned to her. "Catherine, I'd like you to meet Tiana Spencer." With an
inclination of his glossy head, he concluded, "Tiana,
Catherine Hunter."

Tiana's lips felt like the thickest molded clay as she
forced herself to respond to the brief introduction. She
should have realized that a man like Bayne Dahlquist
would only appear with the *crème de la crème* of female
society. Hazily, Tiana recalled reading somewhere
that Catherine Hunter was the long-time girlfriend
of an advertising tycoon. Now with a resounding
thud, she knew the nameless tycoon must, in fact, be
Bayne.

Catherine Hunter, the epitome of sophistication,
issued a greeting which reaffirmed her station without
lessening her dramatic image. "Can I call you Tiana? It
is such an extraordinary name."

"Of course, and thank you," Tiana murmured
woodenly, held in a mysterious grip of paralysis.

"Please call me Catherine." The model spoke with a
lilting throatiness. "Peter told me he had just hired you
as his assistant today. Working with him is a dream.
However, you must learn to tolerate his one little fault.
Peter assumes everyone is as dedicated as he is. I bet he
has you working tonight and you aren't even on the
payroll yet!" She chuckled huskily, concealing nothing
of her basic femininity.

"I don't mind." Tiana smiled automatically. "I was
thrilled at the chance to come to the opening tonight."

Bayne scoffed, "Undoubtedly, you look upon tonight
as a great adventure and not work."

"Not an adventure! But not work either!" Tiana

retaliated with more vehemence than was necessary. Within scant moments of their meeting, Bayne had goaded her into losing her control, spurred her to say things she would not have under other circumstances. Mentally, Tiana wagered that he would not have dared to bait her if she had resembled someone as polished and poised as Catherine Hunter. But no amount of wishing could alter the present. She was not like the model. Embittered, Tiana could only pray that with the passage of time, Bayne would trust less in his first impression of her.

"If you do not consider this work, then surely you are one of the few people here who actually came for the exhibit." Cynicism rebounded in his remark. "The vast majority are here profiling—seeing and being seen by others."

"Is that why you came?" Tiana flared heatedly.

In spite of, or maybe because of, her spontaneous aggression, Bayne snickered, "Would it surprise you if I said yes?"

"Surprise—no." She fixed her eyes on his frankly, not weakening at their inescapable directness. "Disappoint—yes." And then she swallowed as the significance of her words sank into her numbed brain. She had unwittingly spoken the truth!

Simultaneously, Bayne's eyebrows flew upward as if he too was startled by her confession. "You almost make me wish it weren't so," he commented softly, regretfully. But then his eyes narrowed. "If you persist in making declarations like that one, I'll have to start calling you Polly."

Tiana rocked her head sideways, silently questioning.

"Pollyanna!" he supplied.

Tiana could not deaden her response. She flushed furiously. Whether from prodded anger or stinging hurt, she did not pause to ponder as wave upon wave of burning humiliation engulfed her. Tiana tried in vain to save her damaged pride.

"Bayne! How could you?" Catherine exclaimed in astonishment. "You're embarrassing Tiana!" The model lifted her hand from his sleeve.

He scrutinized Tiana's face while answering, "Catherine, this is New York. Surely, you are not being taken in by Tiana's too-sweet face and innocent blushes? She can take care of herself. I have her personal assurance of it."

"Bayne!" Catherine laughed his name. "What has gotten into you? This isn't like you. I think you should apologize."

"You can't blame me because Tiana looks naive and vulnerable. Anyway, she knows the score and there is no need to apologize." Bayne's gaze scorched Tiana's face, bringing fresh color to the surface.

Catherine made a clicking sound with her tongue. "Do you really expect me to believe that Tiana is unmoved? If you want to play games, Bayne, you should at least pick on someone with a greater defense against you."

Smiling wickedly, his eyes never leaving Tiana, Bayne said, "I won't apologize . . . unless she asks me herself."

Never! Not in a million years or a million times a million years would Tiana ask him for an apology! For all her good intentions, Catherine Hunter had merely succeeded in making Tiana's predicament worse. If only Tiana did not react so transparently to him, none of this would have happened. Ultimately, she was shamed under the very mockery she had come to despise. Tiana bowed her head, unable to tolerate his ridicule. "There is no need to apologize."

"You see!" Bayne pointed out to Catherine, a note of undisguised gloating in his voice.

"I see you've had your way again, Bayne," Catherine said, not in the least annoyed.

He laughed, a vividly masculine sound, rich and full of timbre.

It was cold comfort to Tiana that Catherine had restored Bayne to good humor. Perversely, she would have preferred his mood to remain cuttingly cynical than to observe the other woman soothing it. Oddly Tiana felt her feelings of mild annoyance overlaid with a layer of jealousy. She rebuked herself for even giving it a passing thought. Why should she care if the redhead was able to meld and mold into the strength of Bayne when she herself was only capable of grating against his grain? Her eyes veered away from the couple as Catherine's musical peel of laughter enjoined his. Tiana's darkened gaze scanned the crowd, eventually catching sight of Peter, who waved a hand as her smile pleaded with him for rescue. Tiana's eyes desperately clung to him and misted with the supreme effort it took to steady them. But it was useless. Unbelieving, she watched as Peter turned on his heel to snake his way through another bank of people, to disappear from her view. And suddenly, inexplicably, Tiana felt lonely. In spite of the couple so near she felt overwhelmingly alone, virtually isolated, a solitary prisoner of a new-found emotion.

Summoning a plastic smile, shaping it to her stiff lips, Tiana said, "If you will excuse me, I think I'll look at the displays over there." She made a conspicuously vague gesture with the catalog she had rolled in her hand.

"Have you met Lewis Starke yet?" Bayne asked, postponing her flight. A touch of laughter still lingered at his mouth.

"No." An errant tissue of regret hung on the word.

"Catherine and I were about to find him. Why don't

you come with us?" His smile now was friendly and
Tiana could almost believe it was sincere.

But the truth was, Tiana did not want to feel any
more awkward than she already did by attaching herself
to the striking pair. "No, thank you. You two go along
without me."

"Oh, come on, Tiana," Catherine urged, oblivious of
Tiana's desire to escape a situation that had become a
pressing ordeal for her. "It won't take a minute and
you'll have plenty of time to see the rest of the exhibit
later." She spoke quietly but with the cadence of one
used to having her opinions considered and her advice
heeded.

But Tiana was already shaking her head, refusing
Bayne's invitation. An ebony strand of her hair dislodged from the chignon and she was forced to calm her
agitation as she twisted it back into the loose knot.

It was all the opening Bayne needed. "Perhaps Tiana
has her own image of Starke and if she meets him she
would have to reevaluate her opinion and possibly
admit an error." The suggestion was made with a cool
disdain.

"That's not true!" Tiana impulsively cried out,
angered by his unfair judgment against her reasoning.
Then she paled. Belatedly she saw the corner of his
mouth twitch and knew he had adeptly finessed a
reaction from her. The increasingly familiar glint in his
eyes told her without words that he had not meant it. "I
don't want to miss any of the display," Tiana trailed
lamely, aware of how very weak her logic was, after her
impetuous outburst.

"If you don't see it all tonight, you can come again. It
will be up for a week," Catherine pointed out serenely.

Tiana was being successfully maneuvered into ac-
companying them. To continue her refusal might
provoke Bayne further and she was not willing to risk

another encounter so soon on the heels of her last defeat. It did not take a genius to know she was no match for Bayne. Not many women would be.

Once past the drift of viewers, Bayne located the artist in the outer lobby. Lewis Starke stood shrouded in the cloak of austerity, a preoccupied ascetic. A man in his late forties, he had a heavy, brooding gaze to his hazel eyes, a thatch of straw hair tufted rebelliously over his lined forehead, while a thin, nervous smile grazed the line of his mouth.

"Lewis, you must be very proud! The exhibition is an unqualified success," Catherine enthused boundlessly as soon as Bayne had made the introductions.

Tiana echoed a similar sentiment. She could not fail to notice that no amount of praise breached Starke's self-erected shield of uneasiness. His replies were inflexible and stilted, unusual for a man so proclaimed for his daring and freely expressionistic art.

Catherine was not put off by the artist's lack of conversation. She filled the gaps with patterings of inconsequential chatter that were quite amusing. And soon, Lewis Starke lowered his reserve and his smile thawed. Consigned to a non-speaking role, Tiana fastened her attention to the conversation. She could not help but admire the evident ease with which the model spotted the weaknesses in the situation and instinctively compensated for them.

Bayne angled his head toward Tiana and taunted, "You're not bored already, are you?" Obviously uncaring of the proximity of the others, a fiendish mischief danced in his eyes.

"No, no. I find it all fascinating. This is the first opening I've ever attended for a well-known artist," Tiana answered immediately, demonstrating how finely tuned she was to Bayne's presence.

"They are all pretty much the same, which is one

reason why he hates them so much." Bayne tipped his head in the direction of Starke. "But like anything worth having, success too has its price tag."

"Surely someone as famous and gifted as Mr. Starke would not have to attend if he preferred not to come?" Tiana asked with a grit of irritation.

A sinfully contemptuous smile forded Bayne's mouth, bringing a sparkling gleam to his eyes. It nearly caused Tiana's heart to stop beating. Then he said, "You think because Starke is now famous he no longer has to kowtow to anyone?"

Although Bayne's infuriating habit of guising a question as a statement of fact aggravated her to no end, Tiana was compelled to agree in general principle. The short movement of her head gave lie to the mad, erratic fluttering of her heart.

"How long do you think Starke, or anyone else for that matter, would remain at the top without the backing of the people who helped put him there in the first place?" It was a rhetorical question and he carried on. "I can see by your face you think talent should be enough." He threw her a mixed look, half despair, half sorrow. "Well, talent is rarely enough. Fame and acceptance are elusive states at the very best. They are a godless combination of talent, drive, and timing. You can have all the talent you need but without the catalyst of public promotion you will never be recognized. Someday, the human race may have to answer for all the emphasis we have put on the hard sell. But not today, not tomorrow." He sighed, suddenly weary.

"Fame and recognition are not the only worthwhile goals," Tiana said heroically.

"Naturally not, but you will find any activity that transverses those things done strictly for personal need or satisfaction, entails dependency on other people. It is always a trade-off. Where you find dependency, you find compromise. The higher you go, the more you have to give of yourself. Need I say more?" Contempt was barely leashed in the eyes roving so freely over her face. "The first thing to go is, of course, idealism."

His icy, calculating logic washed over her. But she refused to surrender to its numbing effect. Instead she trained her voice with a precision that was foreign to her. "If what you state were always the case, I should think few people would even attempt it."

"Ah, Tiana, how can I convince you, when you see everyone as good and deserving? There are many people who would give anything to achieve a modicum of fame. If they possessed a soul, they would no doubt barter it to the devil."

"Assuming there is a devil." She tried to match the faint boredom in his tone but failed dismally.

"Oh, there is a devil all right." His teeth flashed in a caricature of a smile. "If for no other reason than because people believe there is one."

She could not continue with it. Nothing she did or said would ever convince him. The more she tried to instill a spot of brightness into his bleak outlook, the more she sloughed down further into the bottomless mire of his cynicism. Cutting her losses where they were, Tiana said, "It is obvious we have little if anything in common. I don't want to discuss it any longer."

"As you wish. But ignoring something will not make it go away. Sometime you will have to look at your dreams in the glaring light of reality. You can't have it both ways. Either the dream goes or your idealism does." His head was tilted arrogantly and he glanced down at her with a haughty, supercilious amusement.

"Why do you persist in calling my beliefs idealistic?" she fired back, inflamed by his wounding opinion and by his prejudicial stare. "This is the way I am. It is me! I just can't believe life is as tarnished and soiled as you would pretend it is." Emotion burned up the air in her lungs and she had to suck in a deep breath. "Can't you accept we are different and leave it at that?"

"Your expression is priceless!" Bayne laughed. "Really nothing is as bad as your face leads me to believe you think it is." His eyes were dappled with a teasing light; the green halo growing smaller around the warm, liquid black of the pupil.

Tiana slanted him a curious look before glancing away in confusion. His eyes in conjunction with the deep reverberation of his voice caused her own feelings to crazily tumble one on another until she was incapable of sorting them out. Then like some electronic homing device, her gaze returned to him, catching and holding the flaming glow of his. And for one shattered splinter of time, she was removed from the absolute reality of the situation. She was a woman, without a past, a present, or a future; and Bayne was a man, devoid of complexities and serrating edges. Thus, they stood rooted to one another, transfixed by something older and stronger than all the differences between them.

But then, an involuntary thought came to Tiana. This was no man removed from time and space. This was Bayne Dahlquist! And if she continued to allow herself to react with a lightning anger to him, she would certainly be flirting with the fates. She had not forgotten his warning that she should go back to Georgia. She would not give him any excuse to take away her employment. "I guess I'm not very good at hiding my thoughts. I think it would be better if we steered clear of any discussions about our ideologies."

"Whatever you say. It was never my intention to

distress you, only to warn you." The nameless spirit dwelling in his eyes fled as swiftly as it appeared. The dark center of his eyes constricted as the iris widened to a brittle, chromatic green.

His concession weighted like alum on her tongue. The hard cast to his gaze incited second thoughts. She would be willing to give virtually anything to spark a glinting blaze within his eyes. However, before her wish was more than a fleeting reflection, Peter approached.

Her attention was channeled to the sportive conversational vein as Peter joined Catherine and Lewis. It was plain that yet another sympathetic friend had been added to Starke's retinue by the photographer's arrival.

"I saw our friend Bailey furiously writing in his notebook," Peter announced without reserve. "I asked him what he thought of the exhibit. And he said it was so good, he was going to recommend the entire country be privileged to see it. You know what that means!" Peter nudged the artist with his elbow. "He will call for a traveling exhibit, and whatever Bailey so much as hints at in his column is considered done."

Shaking his head in disbelief, Starke said, "I don't know if I'm up to it."

"Nonsense, Lewis!" Catherine Hunter's considerable charm had moved into a ready intimacy with the artist. "You will only have to make appearances at a few of the larger openings. Think of all the people who will get a chance to see your work, who might not otherwise."

"That's true," Starke conceded as doubt and confidence dueled for mastery of his voice.

"Cheer up, Lew!" Bayne ordered good-naturedly. "It could be worse. You might never have been discovered at all."

Bayne's sly barb was enveloped in responsive laughter. Strangely enough, the humor in combination with Lewis Starke's lack of conviction sliced through Tiana's core of romanticism so that she laughed along with the others.

Then, before she realized what was happening, Peter stepped away from the group and started to take pictures. Even as the brimming laughter mellowed to smiling traces, he continued to press the hissing button. Instinctively, Tiana began to move out of the range of the camera, but her retreat was thwarted as Bayne's arm encircled her waist, fencing her within its intimate range. Startled by his action and by the fevered touch of his body through the layers of her clothing, Tiana tipped her head back to gauge his reaction. But his attention was directed elsewhere, and in any case, the firm, impregnable set of his jaw indicated no revelations would be forthcoming. She sneaked a few seconds to study his unyielding profile before permitting herself to relax as he secured her to his side. Even after Peter had lowered his camera and rejoined the conversation, Bayne kept her anchored there. It must have been an automatic gesture on his part because his proprietorial hold did not loosen when Peter came to her side. Tiana found it necessary to break away from the incomparable temptation of his sheltering body. Not the easiest of tasks.

"Have you seen much of the exhibit?" Peter directed to her with a boyish grin.

"Not as much as I had hoped to see," she admitted honestly, in spite of the witching distraction she felt at the nearness of Bayne. Although he no longer touched her, the imprinted memory of his body against hers raised all manner of havoc with her senses.

"Good! Then you're not in a big hurry to leave. I have a few more people I want to see," Peter said.

"No problem, I would really love to see the rest of the show." Tiana smiled agreeably.

"Sure you don't mind?" Peter's gaze struck out over the heads of the people surrounding them as if already mapping his route in advance of the first step.

"Not in the least."

And whatever else she might have said was lost as Bayne interceded, "Besides, I'll keep her company."

"Great! Then I won't feel like I have to hurry back," Peter called over his shoulder for he was already moving into his travel pattern.

At his untimely desertion Tiana addressed Bayne, "It isn't necessary. I'm perfectly capable of viewing the remainder of the exhibit on my own."

"You object to my going with you?" Bayne asked with a skeptically cambered brow.

Why did he have to put it that way? Tiana did object to his presence but she could never admit to him why. "No, no, of course not." And why did she feel like she was apologizing?

A shadow of a smile slid into place an instant before Bayne reached an arm around Catherine's back. As the model turned to him, he said, "Tiana and I are going to see the rest of the exhibit. Do you want to come?"

"Let her stay with me," Lewis Starke pleaded before Catherine had a chance to answer. "Catherine makes an unpleasant duty so much nicer."

"Go on Bayne. I'll stay with Lewis for a while." The redhead's mouth moved into a perfect smile, broad and exactly high enough so laughter lines did not form around her enchanting eyes.

Tiana tried to mouth a protest but her paltry effort was brushed aside as Bayne escorted her to the other room. And when they reached the first display, Tiana discovered she was no longer capable of voicing an objection. She was in the deadly grasp of some mystical illusion. She had never felt this way before.

Perplexed beyond the reaches of her limited experience, Tiana flipped through the pages of her catalog, burying her concentration in its sleek pages. Anything would be better than facing her undeniable attraction to Bayne. But the fledgling sense of escape afforded by the pages of the book was quickly snatched from her. In one decisive move, Bayne's hand reached across her line of vision, closing the pages as he removed it from her unresisting fingers. And when she might have tendered a cry of protest, he silenced her with the lifting of one cresting brow.

Compressing her lips together in a thin white line, Tiana's eyes lingered on the small booklet held so temptingly out of reach. With its removal, Bayne had eliminated her one excuse for ignoring him. Not that she was fool enough to believe she would have been completely successful with the ruse. Still, by her way of thinking, it had been worth a try. When she raised her eyes, it was to meet the full measure of his glittering mockery.

"I know enough to answer your questions without you putting your nose in a book," he commented with impressive dryness.

And in truth, Tiana soon discovered it was no idle boast. Bayne knew considerably more about the art world in general and Starke's work in particular than the catalog would have conveyed. With informal ease, he tossed around the jargon and theories commonly found only among artists and critics.

As they approached the end of Starke's earliest period, Tiana paused to read the discreetly lettered plate below one of the bolder canvases. Although no sound passed them, her lips formed the words, *On loan from B. Dahlquist.* She turned to him in mute question but the explanation was concealed in his serpentine eyes.

He strode purposefully to the next display, leaving her to make her own way.

Hesitantly, she followed. "It's yours?" Her head canted toward the painting they had just left.

Bayne nodded his head once, a sign of agreement and dismissal conveyed with singular efficiency.

However, Tiana chose to disregard the implied warning. "You're an art collector!"

"No, I have a few pieces but I am not a collector." The desire to conclude the discussion was harbored in his voice.

Wisely, Tiana refrained from the urge to pursue the topic of conversation. But when another plaque bearing his named loomed into sight, it was too much for her. "Do you just collect Starke's work or do you collect other artists as well?"

Furrows of thunder rolled over his forehead. "I am not a collector," he reiterated softly, too softly for safety's sake.

"But obviously, you . . ." Her voice vaporized as she watched the storm clouds scudding across his eyes.

"But obviously, I—what?" He demanded with a deceptive silkiness.

She attempted to strike down the terror threatening to overpower her. "But obviously you have several pieces."

Amazingly, the clouds dispersed as quickly as they had formed. His eyes were once again a calming, jade green. Bayne sighed ponderously, then volunteered, "I have a few items. Some I bought and some were given to me. The only art I have was done by friends. It makes no difference to me whether it personally appeals to me or not. I support the work of a friend."

Tiana was inwardly pleased. She saw Bayne's support of art as far better than those collectors who bought art only as an inflationary hedge, a monetary investment. She beamed at him, the smile a joyous reflection of the thought.

His peaked brows drew down, hooding his eyes. There was a decided pause before he cautioned, "I'm not an altruist. The artwork I own is not the result of good deeds. I simply bought stock in someone's future by giving aid when it was needed. They were business and social investments, ones that are sure to yield dividends."

Her breath caught tightly in her throat as her eyes dimmed a fraction. The meaning of his words could not be denied. Nor could the cynical twist of his mouth.

Tiana and Bayne turned the corner of the last aisle of the exhibition and she took infinite care in keeping her vision averted from him. Her success was practically assured until Bayne's fingers closed gently around the flesh of her upper arm, sending blistering shockwaves of awareness through her body. She was inexorably drawn to him even as her mind shouted its warning not to surrender to this animal attraction. But as her eyes sought his, Tiana discovered it was a groundless fear for his attention was focused above her head to some distant point. Her own gaze was abruptly deflected by the cold impediment of his disinterest.

"Come with me!" His request corresponded to a command.

Before Tiana could finish scanning the room, Bayne was steering her down the length of the aisle, skimming hurriedly past the rest of the displays. Then she saw why he had quickened his pace and her thumping heart somersaulted. Catherine Hunter stood with a middle-aged couple at the head of the last aisle. With a remarkable lack of forethought, Bayne had kept up with Catherine's shifting whereabouts.

All idle wonderings were pushed aside as Tiana was introduced to Martha and George Avery, the older couple talking with Catherine. Tiana soon found out that Mr. Avery was the president of a cosmetic company and Catherine modeled for their Diana line of fragrance. For all the difference in years between herself and the Averys, Tiana immediately felt at ease.

"Peter mentioned you were new in the city," Martha Avery remarked as her delphinium-blue eyes swung in Tiana's direction. Although her dark hair was rivered with white, the older woman's eyes had lost none of their flashing delight. "How long have you been here?"

"Three weeks." Tiana smiled automatically.

"I do hope you intend staying. There is no place on earth like New York City." Martha Avery's merry blue eyes jumped to Bayne. "By the way, how is the campaign coming along?"

With his hands clasped behind his back, Bayne examined the ceiling as if the answer were written above. Finally lowering his head, he chided indulgently, "Martha, you know I'll tell you the minute we have anything definite to relate."

"I know, darling, but I can't help being impatient. I'm so looking forward to getting this campaign under way," Martha said with an infectious gleam in her eyes. "You do remember, George has promised to retire the moment the new line is launched?"

"You won't let any of us forget, Martha," her husband injected good-naturedly. George Avery was a scant few inches taller than his wife. His steel-grey hair sprang back from a pronounced widow's peak in waves so unruly they fought wildly with each other for dominance. His face was tinged with spots of florid

color while his eyes were a somewhat muddied brown
behind wire-frame glasses.

Martha tapped her husband's arm playfully, the
touch changing to an affectionate caress as her hand
rested familiarly on his sleeve. "This is one promise I
mean to have you keep, love. You have been putting
off your retirement for much too long."

"The day the new line officially goes out," George
Avery accorded.

As she continued to stroke her husband's arm,
Martha addressed Bayne, "You do remember our
specifications, don't you?"

"Have I ever failed you?" Bayne countered amicably.

"No-o-o," Martha drew out the word on a fine wire.
"But I am a little anxious about this one. I don't mean
to rush you, but I can't help being impatient. This is
always the worst time for me . . . the waiting." Her
eyes slid to Tiana momentarily before reconnecting
with Bayne's. "I thought you might have something to
discuss."

Bayne had followed the fluid motion of the older
woman's possessive eyes. Wearily, he made a negative
sound deep in his throat, which roughened as his gaze
returned to Martha.

"Are you quite sure?" Martha asked with a designing
narrowing of her eyes.

"Quite!" Bayne snarled, unfairly flicking a sharp
look of irritation at Tiana.

"Martha, leave the poor boy alone," George me-
diated.

The mental picture of Bayne Dahlquist as anyone's
"poor boy" caused Tiana to suppress the smile threatening to overtake her expression. True, it was only a
figure of speech, but the absurdness of it prompted her

to press her lips together in order to swallow the rising giggle. Tiana might not have won, had Bayne's piercing eyes not leveled unmercifully on her. She diverted her gaze but not quickly enough to entirely escape the quelling effect.

"Bayne knows how I am!" Martha stated without apology.

"We all know how you are!" George threw in jovially.

Catherine's laughter peeled out, spilling over the group in a whispering sheet of harmony. The others joined in the humor and Martha seemed to enjoy it most of all.

As the laughter melted to smiles, Martha's eyes darted to Tiana. She lowered her voice. "Tiana, would you mind coming with me to the powder room? I think we can leave Catherine to entertain the men." Her twinkling eyes circled the small group, a glint of mischief in their depths.

Without hesitation, Tiana agreed. As they made their way through the display room and the outer lobby, Martha questioned Tiana about her background and interests. Only after they were seated side by side in front of a long vanity mirror, did the older woman offer an opinion. "You have such expressive eyes, my dear." Martha paused, about to retouch her lipstick. Her eyes met and held Tiana's in the mirror. "In fact, your whole face is expressive. Tell me, have you ever considered modeling?"

Tiana shook her head, her hands busily checking the knot of her hair. Her fingers gathered loosened ends and resecured them with metal hairpins. "Actually no. I have done some posing for friends while I was in art school but nothing professionally."

"Hmmm," Martha acknowledged, pressing the tube of crimson color to her lips. Then as she twisted the lipstick and replaced its cover, she observed, "You are a little under the usual height. What are you, about five foot six?"

"About." Tiana curled a tendril of her silky black hair around her index finger and then repositioned it against her cheek.

"But you are slender and your bones are long so they might photograph well." Martha pressed a folded tissue to her lips, blotting off the excess color.

"I really have no interest in modeling. I came to New York to pursue a career in art, and although working as Peter's assistant isn't exactly what I had originally hoped to be doing, it is close enough." Tiana rummaged in her evening bag. Her fingers pulled out her lip gloss.

"I know the story," Martha chuckled.

Startled, Tiana stopped to glance at Martha in the surface of the mirror.

"Let's say, I've heard it before." Martha patted her primly coiffured hair and smiled knowingly. "Catherine, for one, never intended to model. I've known Catherine for almost ten years." The blue eyes dimmed fractionally in memory. "It has been a good ten years for all of us. I think Bayne and Catherine would have to agree, though neither of them followed the path they had first chosen."

Curiosity raised Tiana's brow.

Glancing down at the diamond-studded watch on her wrist, Martha said, "Would you like to hear a little about how we got together?"

Nodding eagerly, Tiana could barely keep the excitement from showing. She would like to know something about the Averys. They gave every indication of being very nice people. But her real interest lay in gathering some knowledge of Bayne. She knew so little about him and found him so fascinating. Never before had Tiana felt such a pull to another individual. It was a seeking, a yearning, a wanting that cried out to be satisfied. Perhaps Martha would impart some piece of information to ease the hunger of Tiana's spirit. Carefully, Tiana unscrewed the cover of her lip color, her eyes demurely down.

"George and I started in the cosmetic business some twenty-five years ago. For the first fifteen years or so, we barely eked out a living, but we stuck with it because it was what we wanted to do. Then George got an idea for a revolutionary new fragrance line and had a chemist work up the basic scent formula. We envisioned it for a coming generation of women and named it Diana. We loved our idea and believed it would be right for the times but we were faced with the very real problem of marketing it. Now we were a small company at the time and had no contacts to speak of, locally or on the national level. But we decided to gamble everything and go with national advertising. We wanted an exclusive model who would only be identified with our fragrance so that the public would readily identify with the new concept. We simply could not afford what the modeling agencies had, so we asked one of our secretaries to help us. Carol said yes, but her fiancé put his foot down. That headstrong young man was Bayne!"

Tiana's eyes widened as she looked up. So Bayne had been engaged. Had he also been married? Swiftly she returned her eyes to the lip gloss, adopting a nonchalance she was far from feeling.

"I met Bayne when I went to talk to him about allowing Carol to accept the job. They were planning to be married after he finished writing his novel. He refused to allow her to support him, nor would he marry her without being able to support her. Bayne was so unyielding in those days. There was nothing middle-of-the-road about him. He was quaintly and persistently against Carol modeling." Martha took a breath. "Anyway, I finally managed to convince him that George and I desperately needed Carol and he reluctantly agreed. Unfortunately, when Carol went to a photographer for some preliminary pictures, she met a promoter. Before we knew what had happened, Carol became involved with the promoter and they were off to Italy to make a western movie. Needless to say, it left us without a model and Bayne without a fiancée."

Amazed, Tiana's mouth opened in shock. She snapped it shut with such force her teeth clicked together in protest. How was it possible for a woman to leave Bayne . . . tantamount to jilting him? Tiana could not comprehend it.

Martha glanced at Tiana. "I can assure you, it's true. When I heard what had happened, I went right over to Bayne's apartment. I still shudder to think of it. Bayne had destroyed his manuscript and all his notes, determined to leave everything from that time in his life behind. His devastation had carved a resolve in him that defied compromise. But Bayne's great creative drive was intact and he channeled it all into helping us. He revamped the Diana campaign and found us a new model. That was when Catherine entered our lives. She had been working in an office during the day and doing typing for Bayne in the evenings. Bayne was the one who saw her potential and gave her the style that has become Catherine Hunter to the world. He even changed her name and fabricated a background that would give her allure and mystery. At the time we never dreamed Catherine would go so far or that the Diana line would become so successful. As they say, the rest is history. We became the sixth largest cosmetic company in the country."

Tiana filled in the rest for herself. Bayne went on to become an advertising entrepreneur and Catherine became one of the top models in the world. His Pygmalion to her Galatea; a vignette played in the tempo of Madison Avenue. Tiana closed the top on her lip color and slipped it back into her purse. With downcast eyes, she murmured, "Thank you for telling me."

Not much later, Martha and Tiana located the others exactly where they had left them. And it was not much past that when Martha suggested to George that it was time they leave.

Although Catherine and Bayne accompanied Tiana as she viewed the remainder of the display, she found the artwork no longer possessed the power to recapture her interest. Her thoughts were elsewhere, musing over the relationship that had developed between Catherine and Bayne in the near decade they had known one another. Finally, after what seemed an eternity to Tiana, they reached the last item of Starke's work.

Politely, Bayne asked, "Is there anything else either of you would like to see?"

"No, I've seen enough!" Catherine avowed.

"Tiana?" Bayne inquired.

"No, nothing else, thank you," she refused. Suddenly every second spent in the company of Bayne and Catherine vibrated Tiana's nerves so each one pulsed and throbbed in a cacophony of unnamed emotion.

"Do you want me to find Peter?" Bayne asked blandly, surveying her features with an uncritical eye.

"I'll find him myself," she told him tartly and then questioned her own reply.

His one scarred brow cocked skeptically. "I can save you the trouble. I think I saw Peter through the archway."

Chastised, Tiana followed meekly as Bayne led the

way to the outer lobby. And before she was fully aware
of it, Peter was in front of her, claiming her attention
and occupying her thoughts so they no longer dwelled
so perversely on the auburn-headed man and his
partner.

"I'm about finished; been waiting long?" Peter
capped the fitted lens cover on his camera.

"No," Tiana spoke up, unduly happy at not being the
third wheel any longer.

"Good! How about stopping for a drink? Bayne?
Catherine?" Peter asked as he slung the camera over
his shoulder.

With a sinking sensation, Tiana watched as a silent
message was telegraphed between Bayne and Catherine. A pain in her chest tightened as she saw the way
they came to agreement without uttering a sound. They
were so close, so obviously attuned to one another,
words were not necessary.

Catherine voiced the answer for both of them. "Fine,
but let's not make it too late."

"There is a place around the corner. We can walk
from here," Peter announced.

From the sidewalk, the club appeared to be smaller
than it was on the inside. It was a long, extremely
narrow room with a bar running the length of one wall.
Stained-glass windows and a turn-of-the-century decor
conflicted with the blaring music and steaming bodies
packed within the walls. Miraculously, Peter found a
table for them in the back, no easy feat considering
people were stacked three-deep at the bar. The noise
level practically forbade any attempt at conversation
and for the most part they drank their cocktails in
silence, leaving after one drink apiece.

When they reached the pavement, Tiana realized her
eyes were smarting from the thick smoke they had left
in the room. Wiping away the moisture collecting in the

corners of her eyes, she glanced up overhead. It was a close, heavy night. The sky was starless and hazy as a veil of humidity settled over the city. Somewhere up there was a moon but it was no longer visible. Peripherally, Tiana was aware of Peter's arm around her shoulder and took advantage of his guidance by looking up at the tall buildings surrounding them, monochromatic in the artificial light. Peter accepted Bayne's offer of a ride home and so they walked to the garage where he had left his car.

Street parking in her neighborhood of SoHo, like the rest of the island-borough of Manhattan, was a rarity. So it was only routine courtesy that prompted Tiana to ask if they would like to come up for coffee. Bayne and Catherine refused; he with laconic thrift, she with effusive regret. However, Peter did accept her invitation.

After Bayne double-parked his car, Peter uncurled his lanky frame and liquidly got out of the car. Holding the door for Tiana, he leaned into the door space and said, "Thanks a lot! See you Monday!"

Casually, Tiana added her thanks to his before sliding across the expanse of seat to stand beside Peter. They reached the top of the outside steps of her building when she heard the car purringly change gears. She turned in time to see its glowing taillights as it accelerated from her view.

Inside her cramped apartment, Peter occupied himself by looking through some of her canvases while Tiana brewed the coffee. He made no comment until he stopped before the half-completed painting on the easel. "Who is sitting for you?" He took a side step, altering his perspective, his fair head tilted in thought.

"No one. It's a memory composite," she tossed over her shoulder before reaching for two hand-crafted ceramic mugs. She poured the coffee. "Since then, I've decided to rework it and lighten up some of those shadows. Cream? Sugar?"

"Negative to both," Peter answered and then walked toward her to lift the cups from her hands. He placed them on a convenient table, ignoring her questioning eyes. Within a split second, his hands came to rest on her slim shoulders, his thumbs gently trailing along the hollowed curve of her collar bone. His arms held her at length while he studied her upturned face.

Tiana's heart pounded in her breast. Peter's nearness, his touch, had nothing to do with it. He was about to make a pass and she did not want him to follow through. Without a doubt, he was experienced and he had the added influence of having hired her that very day. Still, she did not relish the position of having to rebuff his advances.

There was a glistening glimpse of white teeth before he pulled her purposefully toward him. The cincture of his arms, as they wrapped around her, sealed the action with an unmistakable intent.

Instinctively, Tiana ducked her head, directing it to nestle beneath his chin. She found the growth of his beard soft as it brushed lightly against her temple. She did not find his closeness repulsive, only awkward.

Peter leaned away from her as his fingers came up to tip her chin. Her eyes were forced to meet his unwavering gaze. "I want to spend the night." Lowering his head, his mouth was poised intimately above hers, awaiting her decision.

The meaning of his statement clawed at her self-possession. It was too forthright, too blunt, to ever be confused with the youthful pleading and teasing she had known in the past. She lodged her hands against his chest and broke the confining embrace. It was an involuntary gesture borne of her reaction to his frank proposition.

"No?" he probed as his hands pliantly maintained a superficial contact at her waist.

"No!"

"Take it easy." He released her completely. "It's no big deal, you know!"

"It is for me."

"Unusual," he observed with dilatory candidness. His eyes, although a flat earthen brown, delved into her harried composure. But then a rueful smile hooked the corner of his mouth. "You can't blame a guy for trying."

Her tongue nervously moistened her dry lips as she searched for some hidden meaning, some ulterior design. She clearly remembered the way Peter had responded to Bayne's cynicism after the interview with noncommittal tolerance that may have been more than idle familiarity. Peter might expect something in return for the job he had given her. Did her employment hinge in any way on his suggestion? She had to find out. "Does this mean . . ." Her voice dissolved in abject misery, unable to form the words of the question gnawing within her.

"It means nothing!" Peter dismissed her concern without hearing the question.

But she was not satisfied. Bayne had planted hateful thoughts in her mind. She had nothing in her experience with which to deal with them. Finding no other way, Tiana blurted, "Will this have any effect on my job?"

"Don't be silly!" came his censorious reproof. His annoyed expression laid down amusement with the criticism. "Look here, Tiana, I admit I hired you on a hunch. I'm an intuitive person. But you do have talent. I would not have taken you on otherwise. I wanted to stay the night because you are a desirable woman. As far as I'm concerned, one thing has nothing to do with the other." He emphasized with a Gallic thrust of his hand. "Now that it is out in the open, neither of us will have cause to wonder in the future about imagined or real possibilities. The other is nice, but so is the ease that comes with working with someone when there is nothing physical. Much more practical all the way around."

Grave assention outlined her rounded eyes, darkening the edges to an umber rim of color. It was a cut-and-dried explanation sans any romantic overtones. But it did assure Tiana that her position with Peter would not be influenced by the personal. She could easily live within that parameter. Smiling broadly, she greeted the pact with glowing relief. "I would really like that, Peter!"

"But I don't want you to feel you can't change your mind if the spirit moves you." Peter aped a beguiling leer before retrieving his mug from the table. He consumed a goodly portion of its contents before saying, "You know, Tiana, I never actually expected you to let me stay the night."

"You didn't?" Her voice climbed with doubt.

Peter shook his head. "No, but don't think I wouldn't, given half the chance." He chuckled with lascivious mischief. "You have this incredible look of solemn innocence with just a suggestion of impishness lurking in the shadows of your eyes. I wasn't sure if it was something real or something manufactured. And now I know!"

The explanation was so similar to Bayne's opinion of her and yet there was a wide world of difference between them. Bayne jeered at her, taunting her until she could not stand it anymore. Peter accepted her innocence as an intrinsic part of her. Why couldn't Bayne be more flexible in his assessment of her? Tiana's eyes migrated from Peter's sympathetic appraisal to rove the room with a restless frustration. Would thoughts of Bayne Dahlquist always intrude where they were not wanted to usurp the place of more comforting ones? Eventually she spied her untouched coffee and was prompted to ask, "Can I get you some more coffee?"

"Nope. I have to be going." Peter replaced his mug next to hers and then reclaimed his camera. "I need to develop these tonight." He held the camera aloft by way of explanation before swinging it onto his shoulder.

Instantaneous comprehension lit Tiana's face. The last stubborn stain of uncertainty was routed from her troubled thoughts. Peter had spoken the truth. He meant what he had said. Their relationship would be strictly fraternal. Confident, Tiana teased, "And what would you have done if I had decided to let you stay?"

His grin was devilishly youthful, full of prankish misadventure. "I can always change my plans!"

Even though the backlash of his announcement was charmingly flirtatious, Tiana quickly amended, "No-no! That's all right!"

Peter laughed, his head moving from side to side in fraudulent disbelief. And Tiana smiled, only too grateful to confirm their camaraderie. Peter, at least, would not be any problem to her in the future. Would she ever be able to say that about Bayne Dahlquist? Somehow, Tiana doubted it.

Chapter Three

Unconcealed amazement registered on Tiana's face. She could hardly believe it when a glance at the prominently displayed wall clock in the main workroom of the Dahlquist Agency signaled less than two hours until quitting time. Her first week had been a baptism by fire! But she had no regrets. As a result of the initiation, Tiana felt more like a seasoned professional than the raw recruit she had been on Monday morning.

The vast majority of her time had been taken up doing the precise kinds of errands Peter had indicated would be her assignments: locating props, delivering contracts, and once even picking up Peter's tuxedo from the dry cleaners. It was all so new and exciting that Tiana found little to disillusion her. If she was not actually working as an artist at least she was working around people who were. And on the final day of this, her first week, Peter had loaned her out to the art room. She had pulled the least creative task, nevertheless, lettering posters did put her a step closer to the world she loved.

Directing her attention to the chore at hand, Tiana finished drawing the final outline on the italic lettering. At long last, she had completed all the posters.

Calligraphy was not her forte and it did not take much for the tedium to set into her bones. She snapped the cap on the marker and slowly, painfully straightened her back. Arching her spine, she reached a hand around to massage the lower portion where stiffness had cast its troublesome shadow. Thoughtlessly, she had not considered the tension and time involved and so had not taken a stool to sit on while bending over the drafting table. She would know better the next time.

"Finished?"

Without bothering to look around, Tiana knew it was Peter. Her hands were again occupied with the routine task of putting away her drawing equipment and clearing the work space. "I didn't think you would be back today."

"Neither did I!" he quipped. "But I remembered something I had planned to get done this week."

"What was it?" she asked, only partially interested in his answer. Tiana stretched to grasp the last marker on the slanted surface as it began to roll in the opposite direction.

"Something I want you to do for me. Come to my office when you're finished here."

Intrigued, Tiana raised her head, managing to catch a glimpse of his departing back. She was tempted to call out to him but thought better of it. She would find out what awaited her soon enough.

Before she could leave the work area Tiana had to spray all the posters with a fixative in order to protect her work. After setting the posters in a drying rack, she ran headlong into one of the illustrators, who asked her to fetch him some supplies from the storeroom. It would delay her but Tiana felt compelled to do it without offering an excuse. She liked working in the art room and did not want to jeopardize her chances of returning. However, it took more than fifteen minutes to locate the right size clamps and Tiana was breathless by the time she rushed into Peter's office.

"I'm sorry to be so late," she apologized.

"Not to worry! Are you free now?" Peter replied as he continued to pack an attaché case with papers and folders.

Her brow wrinkled as her mind scooted back over the events of the day. "I think so!"

"Good, then let's get going!" Peter snatched up the leather case and tucked it under one arm as he headed for the door with a quickening gait.

Peter obviously intended for her to follow him so Tiana asked with a candied frosting of humor, "Can I ask where we are going?" But even as she spoke she was hurrying to collect her handbag.

Evasively, Peter responded, "All in good time—come on!"

To her intensifying curiosity, she discovered Peter had no intention of enlightening her. He set about his mission with a single-minded fervor that did not happen to include a discussion of his plans with her. Her heels doing double time to his loping walk, Tiana pursued him out of the office building to a department store, where he bought a pair of black tights and a dancer's leotard, propitiatorily telling the salesclerk they were for Tiana and to size them accordingly. Tiana's eyes widened but she said nothing. Instead she shot Peter a questioning look but received no answer. Even when he unceremoniously deposited her in a taxi, she was unable to ferret out the meaning of their destination, as he provided the cabbie with a low-numbered address on St. Luke's Place.

The taxi negotiated the orderly gridiron pattern of the midtown streets to enter the whimsically arrayed ones of Greenwich Village. As they turned into St. Luke's Place, Tiana saw remarkably well-preserved

houses in the Italiante styling that had become synony-
mous with the famed New York brownstone. Still,
Peter kept his silence.

Internally wrestling with the dilemma Peter had
presented, Tiana renewed her promise not to nag for
some answers to her questions. Who had he bought the
costume for and where were they going? And more
importantly, why? Fortunately for her dwindling willpower, she did not have to remain in suspense long.

As the cab left them off in front of one of the charmingly aged brownstones, Peter announced, "We're
home!" It went without saying, he meant his home, for
Tiana had never in her life been on St. Luke's Place.

Inside the house, Tiana saw it was tastefully and by
no means inexpensively furnished along contemporary
lines accented with compatible antiques. With an
abrupt wave, Peter directed her into the living room
while he disappeared down the hall toward the back of
the house. He called out for her to make herself at
home.

Remaining mystified, she did exactly as he directed
by walking along the photograph-laden walls of the
room. The photographs were excellent and she began
to realize the scope of Peter's talent. As her eyes
surveyed the variety, Tiana could not even measure the
full extent of his expertise.

"Let's sit down." Peter's voice sent Tiana pirouett-
ing. "Did I startle you?" He smiled guiltily. "I am
sorry. Please sit down so we can talk."

She obediently sat down in a comfortable-looking
arm chair but Peter kept standing. His face was sober,
his eyes steady, and he reminded Tiana of an attorney
about to sum up his case before the jury.

"May I be frank with you?"

Vigorously, Tiana nodded her head, willing him to
continue.

"Without going into a lot of detail, I brought you here to photograph you. It shouldn't take more than an hour or two," he stated brusquely.

"You are a fine photographer, Peter. I've just been admiring your work, but I would rather not pose."

"Why not?" Clearly, he had not expected a refusal.

"I posed once or twice for friends and was never comfortable with it. I guess I prefer being behind the easel." The truth filtered through with a sincerity that could not be denied.

"But you posed for painters!" He snubbed her reasoning. "Photography is more active for the model. Anyway, it's only for a couple of hours. Surely, there's no harm in that?" His sagacity tried to brush away her objections.

But something held her back. "I don't know!" The ends of her mouth depressed.

"As a friend?" came his deceptive cajolery.

"Peter, you're not fair," she scolded with an unaccustomed frown.

"Did I ever say I was?" He winked at her, bringing to mind the sweet bonds of their friendship.

In spite of herself, Tiana laughed at his deliberate audacity. "All right, I'll do it! But only this once!" How could she refuse a friend such a small favor?

Afterwards, when she had changed into the leotards and tights, Tiana located Peter in a back room on the first floor. It had been converted into a studio and housed only photography equipment. Peter was adjusting the floor lights when she entered. Despite her soundless steps on stockinged feet, some sixth sense revealed her arrival to him. "Come here so I can check the angle of these lights against your height," he ordered imperiously. This was definitely his realm and here he was the uncrowned king!

Self-consciously, Tiana did his bidding. Peter gave

her no more than a cursory glance as he positioned her
and made minor changes in the lighting, verifying it
with a meter. Tiana grew warm as the lights beamed
brightly over her. It might have been the heat but more
likely it was her nervousness surfacing. She could feel a
thin sheen of moisture rapidly collecting on her brow.
Inadequacy pecked at the crumbling facade of her
poise. She struggled to maintain her composure as she
wiped a hand across her forehead. Then the same hand
circled her neck to lift the heavy weight of hair from
where it lay plastered against her damp skin. Suddenly
the black form-fitting costume seemed too clinging,
much too revealing of her softly rounded curves.

"You're not nervous?" Peter asked as he loaded film
into his camera.

"You want to bet?" Her gaze darted around the
room, apprehensively eyeing the studio equipment.

"Relax! Don't worry! I'll do all the work," he
assured her. "I'll put some music on the stereo. Then
all you have to do is listen to the music and change
positions when I tell you to change." He matched the
action to the promise and in seconds the air was filled
with the strains of a soothing instrumental.

Actually once into it, Tiana found posing was a great
deal easier than she had anticipated. Heartened by
Peter's sympathy, she conscientiously followed his
directions and learned it was like dancing only with
indulgent stops between the separate moves. Occasionally, Peter would say amusing little things, effectively
serving to keep her mind from dwelling on the sibilant
hissing of the camera.

Finally, Peter announced, "That's it! Not too bad,
was it?" A grin tore at the corner of his mouth as he
slanted her a look.

She crinkled her nose as she pretended to give it

careful thought. "Not too bad. Now can I change back into my clothes?"

"Not yet! I want to develop these first to see how they turned out. I may want to take some more." Fresh authority crackled in his voice. "Why don't you go to the kitchen and fix us something to eat while I take care of the film?"

Her brow knit. "Like this?" Her arms akimbo, Tiana tipped her head in pert question.

He scrutinized her as if seeing her attire for the first time. "Wait a sec!" And in three steps he was out of the room. However, Peter managed to return before she had a chance to miss him. He tossed her a tailored man's shirt in pale blue cotton. "Here! You can wear this!"

She caught the shirt and then slipped it over her shoulders. She realized it must be one of Peter's, judging from the styling, an old one. Buttoning the front she saw it came to below midthigh, and the long sleeves had to be rolled several times in order to allow her hands their ordinary freedom.

"Now, if you're all settled, will you get to the kitchen and make yourself useful? Steaks are in the freezer. The oven is microwave, so you can defrost before you grill. The grill is built into the top of the range. If you have any trouble there is an instruction book in the cabinet next to the refrigerator. Give me a call when you're ready!" Peter issued the orders with an infuriating detachment as he retreated again.

"And what if I can't cook?" Tiana called out as he disappeared. She was slightly miffed in being so summarily relegated to kitchen duty. He could have asked.

Although she could not see Peter, Tiana heard him chuckle before shouting. "If you really can't cook, then do the best you can. There should be some bread and cold cuts for sandwiches." His voice carried from behind the closed door across the hall.

Scoffing her dissatisfaction, Tiana pivoted on her heel and went to the kitchen. And since she did know how to cook and was indeed hungry herself, she went about preparing the meal with organized dispatch, even to the point of adding a three-bean salad and asparagus to the steak entree Peter had ordered.

Absently, she hummed along with the music she could hear playing faintly in the background. It was not necessary to call Peter when dinner was ready. He timed his arrival to coincide with the completion of the meat on the grill.

He hovered directly behind her as Tiana removed the steaks from the heat. Hanging over her shoulder, he sniffed the air in robust appreciation. Then with proper relish, he exploded, "You're a good kid!"

She motioned him to sit down at the table, all the while thinking about Peter's buoyant charm. One could simply not be irritated with him for very long. In all probability, Peter could coax a smile from a marble statue without half trying. After they had started eating, Tiana asked, "How did the pictures turn out?"

He waited before answering then said, "Okay, I guess. But don't change yet, I want to make some enlargements first."

Tiana's mobile mouth jutted out in the tiniest possible pout. "Why do you want these pictures anyway?"

Lackadaisically, he lifted his rangy shoulders in a shrug. "No particular reason. You were in some pictures I took at Starke's opening the other night and a few of them were exceptionally good. I wanted to see if they were flukes or if you really do photograph with a certain astral presence."

"With what?" Her otherwise wide eyes narrowed in a perplexed squint.

He smiled briefly before taking a deliberate bite of food and then chewing it well. He finally commented, "It's difficult to explain fully. Each photographer sees something different and each has his own way of describing it. For instance, I used the term astral in referring to you. Another photographer might have said it was innocence and still another might have said it was youthful expectancy. However one goes about describing it, you do seem to have a style all your own that the camera occasionally picks up and reveals. It happens that way sometimes."

"I see." But she really didn't at all. Instead of pursuing it further, Tiana chalked it up to artistic freedom on Peter's behalf and let it go at that. Peter communicated so effectively through the printed form of his art that one could not expect more. However before Tiana could change the subject, Peter bolted the last of his food and excused himself, leaving her to finish her own meal in solitude.

Tiana cleared away the dishes from the table when she was done eating. She washed the dishes and was putting away the last pan when the doorbell chimed. Even before Peter shouted for her to answer it, she was padding lightly along the carpeted hall to the door.

Gracefully, Tiana leaned forward against the door, aligning her eye with the small view lens. She could see out without being observed. Then she froze, motionless, as she peered directly at the unyielding profile of Bayne Dahlquist! She had not seen him since the opening at the gallery but time had not lessened her innate memory of him. Her eyes greedily fastened on him until Bayne was forced to ring the doorbell again, sending Tiana stumbling back on unsteady legs. Immediately, she unlocked the door and flung it open.

With an implacable coolness his eyes settled on her. If he was surprised to see her there, he did not so much as hint at it with a change in his expression. Instead, with a curt, almost cavalier dip of his auburn head, he greeted her. "Hello, Tiana. Will you tell Peter I'm here?"

Wordlessly, she stepped aside so he could pass in front of her. As she replaced the lock, Tiana became acutely conscious of her clothing. It was stupidity itself to feel so exposed, so vulnerable. But logic could not dissuade her. True, every centimeter of her body was unfailingly covered from neck to toes but an odd feeling of discomfort persisted. Her eyes anxiously cut across the distance she would have to travel to carry out his request. She moistened both of her tightly dried lips before she replied, "Of course. Would you like to wait in the living room?"

The movement of his head might have been one of assent if it had not been strangely arrested before its completion. With a metronomically slowed gaze, Bayne's eyes combed the length of her body. His peaked brows arched skyward as he favored her with a universally masculine inspection. He apparently was no Spartan; he took his pleasure where and when he found it. The black fire in his pupils spread so only a slender halo of color surrounded them like foaming green water.

The thoroughness of his visual assault left a wandering bead of trepidation in the pit of her stomach. Despite her best effort, her voice was strangled as she said, "I'll . . . I'll tell him." She did not hesitate but sped past him on boneless legs.

Having delivered the message to Peter, Tiana desperately wished she could remain secreted in the back of the house. She wanted to stay protected by space from the unsettling and altogether disturbing influence of Bayne Dahlquist. The passage of a week had not diluted the primitive, nearly uncontrollable attraction he held for her. But sanctuary was denied her when Peter told her to relay a message and to mix Bayne a drink. Rallying her fleeting courage, Tiana returned to the living room only to find it had not been strictly necessary. Bayne already had a drink in hand and was lounging dispassionately on the couch. Too late to retreat, Tiana caught him looking at her as she stood uncertainly in the entrance. "Peter said he would be a few more minutes. He also told me to get you a drink but I see you managed on your own." It did not escape her notice that Bayne was more at ease in these surroundings than she was. It was he and not she, who knew where the liquor was stored.

Holding the glass of shimmering amber liquid up, Bayne inquired, "Are you having one?"

"No, thank you." Tiana remained rooted to the spot with a growing insecurity. Her eyes clung to his as she watched his vision meander carelessly over her. But with the glass pressed to his lips, she was unable to read his expression with any degree of accuracy. She was only aware of the warmth of his gaze as it drifted seductively down the length of her body. Something imprinted in the shadows of his eyes caused her throat to constrict inexplicably. Her legs became weighted as the blood seemingly pooled within them and she was left giddily lightheaded.

"Why don't you sit down and keep me company?" He had lowered the glass from his mouth, cradling it between his hands.

At his steadily spoken words, Tiana made her way to the nearest chair. She could not help but acknowledge the welcome feel of a solid surface beneath her. She was not at all sure how much longer she could have remained standing in the discerning line of his scrutiny.

"So, how do you like working at the agency?" he questioned straightway.

"I like it! I've only been there a week, but so far I like it!" Thankfully, this was a safe zone of discussion and she silently applauded the firmness of her voice.

"Is it what you had expected?" he continued with consummate skill.

"I honestly never thought about it," she admitted reluctantly. "I suppose it must be, since I feel so comfortable at the agency."

His eyes were skeptical, reflecting glimmering shards of unadulterated green. "I would have thought a girl like you would have been disillusioned about some of the Madison Avenue hard-sell and the media-hype in advertising. Perhaps with a little more time . . ." He left it unfinished as he craftily lowered his thick lashes to take another swallow of his drink.

His words razored into her heart like no other sentiment had ever done in the past. Again she was brutally reminded of his cynical opinion of her and the knowledge hurt like no idle fantasy ever could. It was a searing pain which defied explanation. But unbelievably, a spark of a defensive instinct burned and Tiana sought to cauterize the wound Bayne had so unthinkingly inflicted. "Has it ever occurred to you, I might possibly be something other than what you think I am?"

His erupting laughter belittled her defense more cruelly than anything he could have said. And then, when he did speak, a fractious smile held his mouth. "To tell you the truth, Tiana, the thought never entered my mind. You are an anachronism, a person who should have lived in some bygone era when naiveté was esteemed and honored and not now, and certainly not in New York where you are so much at odds with the environment."

The knife had gone deeper, gouging, cutting; it had brought mountainous waves of unbearable suffering. She was as much an alien to him as if she had been transported from another planet. In a voice as fragile and hollow as a reed, Tiana said, "You are entitled to your opinion. I can only ask you not to hold your prejudices against me."

The net effect of her plea tapered the corners of his eyes. "And exactly what is that supposed to mean?" The customary cynicism had returned to lace his voice.

Her beseeching eyes searched his for compassion; finding none, she spoke with a fortitude she did not recognize. "It means we are different. I have no quarrel with that. But must you throw up our differences—my difference from you—every time we meet? Can't we coexist peacefully?"

The last shred of jeering cynicism fled as Bayne said in an intoxicating whisper, "Peace? Can a man and woman ever coexist in peace when drumfire vibrates through their bodies and frustration rides their spirits?"

And something within her came alive as the sonorous magic of a master sorceror enchanted her, driving away every conceivable thought but one. There was something between them; something not defined with mere words and phrases. It superseded the ordinary and was as elusive as a dream on the wing. Was peace too much to expect? "I ask so little."

"You ask too much!"

Despair and bewilderment crisscrossed her brow. "Is it too much to ask that you refrain from condemning me, ridiculing me, every time we meet?" Her voice caught on a silent sob.

"No. Is that what you were asking?"

His voice had deepened, sending a rolling barrage of incalculable emotion through Tiana. She could only nod her head, having gone past the point of speech.

"All right, I won't criticize you anymore, if that's what you want. But for the record, I never ridiculed you." There was a brief gleam of even white teeth before Bayne added, "But not talking about it won't make it go away. You're living in an ivory tower, if you think it will!"

Her lips clapped together in a straight line. He was impossible! Stricken, she glared at him, not believing Bayne could be so insensitive, so callous. She felt the full, unshielded strength of his gaze on her.

Amusement glittered in his eyes as surely as the remorseless smile turning his mouth. "I've made you angry?"

Yes, but it was the hurt that battled to control her feelings. Tiana absolutely refused to admit he had the ability to evoke such tyrannical emotion within her. She looked away from him, prohibiting him the scene of the intense war taking place. "No!" she answered in cool disdain.

"Haven't I?" he asked quietly.

In spite of a daring effort to the contrary, Tiana's head swung around. One long shiny swatch of her dark hair was sent swimming over her shoulder to lay restlessly on her fluttering breast. "Yes! Yes, you have! Are you satisfied?" With poorly concealed annoyance, one hand flipped the wayward strand back, catching it behind her ear.

The endlessly masculine chuckle rumbling from his throat galvanized not only the sensual curve of his mouth but also the limitless expanse of his compelling eyes.

Oh, she hated him! At that precise moment, Tiana hated Bayne Dahlquist, despised his cynicism and the evil mockery of his smug laughter. Pulling her gaze from his, she seethed with buckling emotion. He was despicable! He was beyond the bounds of redemption—he was . . .

"Tiana?" The whispering of her name from his lips came like silk over velvet.

It was a totally involuntary action when her gaze returned to him. Then it was too late to stop her eyes from flying to his with a magnetic intensity so strong it could have disobeyed the laws of nature had it been required to do so. And it was far too late to prevent her reaction to the devastatingly intimate smile he showered on her.

How was it possible for one individual, one mortal being, to have such total control over the emotions of another? It simply could not be explained. Planned or spontaneous, it mattered not. Bayne had the indisputable talent for stealing responses from her when she had wanted to give none.

"Friends?" Bayne urged unnecessarily; his jaw rose a fraction as if he had reached out to touch her.

"Friends!" she breathed warmly. Her smile met his, matched it, and surpassed it in shoreless joy!

Astonishingly enough, he had done it again. Bayne had successfully played her emotions like a virtuoso practices the musical scales and with about as little effort.

"You must not take everything I say so seriously," he advised smoothly. Soundless laughter brimmed in his voice. "You are so categorically expressive, I find it hard not to tease you."

The luster of her eyes as they trained on him was refracted from her soul. Even his gentle chiding and amusement could not dislodge the radiance from them. Her limited ability to think was hopelessly twined with the feelings threatening to overwhelm her with their sheer variety and force.

"Whoops!" Peter stood in the doorway. "Maybe I should come back later!" His observant eyes shuttled from Tiana to Bayne and back to her.

"You could," Bayne drawled suggestively and Peter took an exaggerated step back in mock obedience.

In extreme haste, Tiana begged, "No, please don't go!"

"Anything for you, hon!" Peter gave her hair an affectionate tweak as he passed by her chair. As Peter yanked open the door of an inconspicuous cabinet, the hidden bar was revealed. "Refill, anyone? Tiana? Bayne?"

"No, thank you," Tiana responded at once. Her harried nerves had reached the overload limit.

"Not for me!" Bayne declined. "I'm on my way to Connecticut for the weekend and only stopped for a minute."

Peter glanced at his watch before replacing the bottle on its shelf. "You might as well stay awhile. Traffic going out of the city now will be murder."

Bayne verified the time with his own watch before he agreed, "You're right about the traffic. I'll stay a little while but don't bother about a refill."

Peter gulped a third of the contents of his glass before crossing to Tiana. Then much to her surprise, he perched his long frame on the armrest of her chair, casually draping an arm over the back of it.

And for the first time since Bayne's arrival, Tiana began to relax as her spine melted into the cushioned padding of the chair. It, likely as not, had something to do with the closeness of Peter. She was comfortable with him, unthreatened by his nearness. Whereas Bayne, who remained at a distance, ignited emotions and feelings that issued warning by their very existence.

After a pause, Bayne volunteered, "After you left

the office Asgard sent back your stuff. I thought you would want to know, Peter."

"All of it?" Peter demanded as his fist pounded into the upholstery of the chair.

"Afraid so," Bayne consoled.

"A hell of a note to start the weekend with, huh?" Peter tipped his glass to his mouth.

"At least this way you know what's waiting for you on Monday morning," Bayne quipped.

"Thanks a lot!" Peter commented with heavy sarcasm.

"You don't want to hear the rest?" observed Bayne dryly.

"There's more?" Peter's eyes were alert, not deceived by Bayne's easy banter.

"Sure is!" Bayne confirmed.

"Then you might as well let me have it," Peter stated resignedly.

"Asgard wants something else by the end of next week."

"You're serious? By the end of next week?" Peter questioned in desperation. "It's impossible!"

"Try telling that to them," Bayne said in mild reproach.

Peter swallowed down the rest of his drink. "I know what you mean! Well, I'll do my best, that's all I can promise you."

"I know you will," Bayne rejoined.

Peter reached across Tiana to place his emptied glass on an end table. As if the action jarred his memory of her, he said, "I just developed some pictures of Tiana. I'd like you to see them, Bayne. Considering she's green, they are fairly good." Peter slanted a look down at Tiana and explained. "It means that for someone with no professional experience in modeling, you're all right." He then shifted his gaze back to Bayne. "Why don't you stay while I shoot another set?"

"Let me see what you have so far." Bayne remained noncommittal about Peter's invitation to stay while he took more pictures.

Peter got up as he said, "Let's go!" With an economy of movement he was out the door, precluding any comments or objections.

Like the gradual uncoiling of a tightly wound spring, Bayne got up. His supremely masculine form towered over Tiana as he inquired, "Coming?"

She watched the play of his tongue against the inside of his mouth and knew instinctively he was forbidding a smile to appear. But the crinkling corners of his eyes undermined his effort and she realized he was laughing at her. Tiana's gaze snapped away from his as she jumped to her feet. With a purposeful toss of her dark hair she passed in front of him, refusing to acknowledge his unspoken taunt. Her back was ramrod straight as he followed her to Peter's darkroom.

Inside the small room, a fine wire ran the length of one wall. A dozen or more negatives were clipped to it. Enlargements were spread out on a worktable. They were all of Tiana, and as she stepped closer she found it difficult to identify with the child-woman of the pictures. She could only account for their gamin quality by a furthering of her respect for Peter's obvious talent of making art out of the ordinary.

Bayne walked slowly along the length of the table, examining each photograph before turning his attention to Peter. He picked up one facial shot of Tiana solemn-eyed and unsmiling. "Not bad."

"But not as good as it could be," Peter said. "Wait here, I want to show you something." Peter left the room and when he reappeared a short while later it was to hand Bayne yet another picture of Tiana.

Bayne studied it. "When was this taken?"

"Starke's opening. I blew it up from one of the group pictures. It's one dynamite picture!" Peter enthused.

Tiana had been forgotten in the conversational shorthand between the two men. It could have been some other girl's pictures they were discussing so abstractly instead of hers.

"Do you think you can do this again?" Bayne handed the photograph back to Peter.

"I don't know but I intend to find out!"

"Now?" Bayne queried.

"Why not?" Peter rejoined rhetorically and left the room.

Resentment billowed in Tiana like helium in a balloon! Had it slipped Peter's mind that she, Tiana Spencer, was posing as a personal favor for him? And not as a professional model at his beck and call. This was all Bayne's fault! She had no intention of posing for Bayne's entertainment! Left alone with him, Tiana glared at Bayne in mutinous rage. She would have said something then but she saw the corners of his mouth twitch meaningfully and could not bear the thought of fueling his warped sense of humor yet again. In a barely disguised huff of temper, she spun from him and stalked out of the room.

In the converted studio Peter was already arranging the lights as they entered. Uncertainly, Tiana stopped only to have the photographer wave her into the room. She was disconcertingly aware of Bayne standing immediately behind her. His nearness, as much as anything else, induced her to move at once into the arc of lights. As she slipped off the blue shirt, there was only the molten fire now burning out of control over every inch of her skin.

Bayne positioned himself against a side wall. His broad back touched it without taking any support from it. His thumbs were casually hooked in the pockets of his fitted slacks. His jacket was open and pushed behind his arms, exposing a widened view of his broad chest.

Summoning her fragmented concentration, Tiana attended Peter's verbal instructions as her eyes broke away from the despotic fascination of Bayne. With him in the room, she was sure every picture taken of her would reveal a stiff, wooden image. How could she possibly relax and be at her best in his electrifying presence when she had never done so in the past?

Tiana had to step to one side as Peter carried over a step ladder and set it up within the circle of lights. The ladder was old and wooden and looked like it had seen better days. After opening the ladder, Peter repositioned one of the floor reflectors and said unequivocally, "Okay, Tiana! Up on top of the ladder!"

"Need help?" Bayne asked without moving from his sedate stance next to the wall.

"No!" she flashed over her shoulder before placing her two hands on the outer frame of the ladder. It wobbled protestingly as she put her weight on the first rung, but with timely forbearance it stabilized as she climbed to the top. The ladder creaked the mildest of complaints as she turned to sit down and then fell silent.

Expecting Peter to issue some sort of directions, Tiana was caught off guard when he immediately started taking pictures. She had no choice but to hastily delegate her meager holding of thought on the task at hand. It was a job not made any easier by the conspicuous lack of music or the nerve-shattering proximity of Bayne. Although the bright glare of the lights prevented her from seeing him in detail, the protective shadows did not blunt her mindful reaction to him. Arousal flared within her like light from a sulphured match.

At last, after what seemed an inordinately elongated span of time, Peter directed, "Now, I want you to stand up on that rung where your feet are positioned."

Automatically Tiana took the order, but upon standing, the ladder began to sway and pitch with an ominous absence of rhythm. Frantically, Tiana searched for something to grasp but her arms only flailed the empty air. However, at the precise instant, she realized she was doomed to tumble forward, the structure miraculously steadied under her. Not needing to look down, Tiana knew it was Bayne who held the base of the ladder and her ankle. His hand squeezed torturously around her ankle bone securing her position with a branding ring of steel. From his touch, flames of intensifying heat radiated upwards with such speed that Tiana feared she would be virtually consumed in a holocaust.

Bayne suddenly released her and then asked, "Are you all right?"

Surprised to discover her equilibrium had returned, Tiana answered shyly, "Yes, thank you." But glancing down and encountering the chromatic green of his upturned eyes was nearly her complete undoing. She thought irrationally the ladder must have lurched again and vowed the earth had shifted on its axis. But she was wrong! The only thing set in motion had been something deep and abiding in the very essence of her.

Peter resumed his picture taking for some uncounted minutes before he called, "Okay, now sit back on the top, knees to the left."

Tiana mechanically obeyed. Bayne made no move to steady her but stepped back behind the scope of the lights; out of her sight but definitely not out of her thoughts. Abstractly, she followed Peter's commands; meanwhile, her mind was busily chaining together impressions of Bayne. With a guilty start, Tiana realized how absorbed she had become with those irascible thoughts as she heard Peter bellow from the dim shadows beyond his camera.

"Here! Catch this!" Peter's disembodied voice cut through the fogging images that had replaced all conscious thought in Tiana's mind.

In vain, Tiana sought to winnow the obscure distance to the source of his voice. But without warning, a white filmy cloth, long and trailing eerily like a comet through the distant night, uncurled on its flight to her.

Heedlessly, she reached out for the material, unquestionably following Peter's directive. Only this time, she had unwittingly engaged danger! Much to her everlasting folly, Tiana found, she had irrevocably upset her precarious balance. Violently the ladder tipped forward and then reared backward as she was unseated. Unthinkingly, her fingers closed over the folds of the ghostly white cloth as her arms went out despairingly to break her impending fall.

Prodigiously, her body was denied the brutal contact with the floor. Instead she met the solid, vividly receptive strength of Bayne as he caught her in his arms.

He took her full weight on impact easily, as if she were no more than a woodland fairy. It seemed to Tiana that he only lowered her to the ground with marked reluctance. But perhaps she was only projecting her unwillingness to leave the haven of his arms. Although her feet touched the floor, Bayne did not take away his support and she took comfort in the welcomed length of his strong body. But despite her gratitude for his timely intercession Tiana could not prevent herself from shivering as the full realization of the near mishap registered.

Responsively, Bayne's arms tightened possessively as he wrapped her closer. With a quiet concern, he whispered above her head. "Are you all right, Tiana?"

And for the second time, Tiana answered, "Yes, thank you! But this time, she said it breathlessly as she snuggled into his tantalizing warmth, not even venturing a glance at him. She felt the gentle patting of his hand on her back as composure gradually seeped into her. As her breathing normalized, Tiana became aware of a disturbing shift from the gentle patting to a languorous stroking as his hand moved in ever decreasing circles. It took no time at all for the significance of her response to dawn on her. With it came a deluge of conflicting feelings. She was inviting insanity if she continued to allow herself to seek solace within his too pleasing embrace! Her body desired the fiery contact while her mind cautioned against the dangers of the emotion exploding within her. Bayne could control more than her moods! He also held power over the fundamental responses of her body!

Breaching her desire, Tiana firmly ordered herself to leave the devilish seduction of his arms. She put her hands against the fabric of his shirt. But with the searing contact of her open palms on the tautened muscles beneath, she almost lost all of her resolve. As if they had a will of their own, her fingers began to curl into the muscular hardness of his chest, defying her wishes. Just in time, she realized what was happening and grasped a new thread of resolution. With a new start and a shuddering sigh, she commanded herself to move.

There was a momentary pressure of his hands and it weakened her determination. The feel, the very male scent of him, threatened to swamp her senses, to rob her of all rational thought. Fighting herself, Tiana's head moved fitfully in a final effort to break through the mystifying charm he held for her. Faintly, as if resisting the shrouding mists of self-denial, she managed, "I'm all right. Really, I am."

"I'm glad to hear it!" The sound vibrated from above and she felt the deliciously delicate movement of his breath on her hair. Something in the mesmerizing timbre stilled her aching spirit. All desire to move had been drawn from her as stealthily and as surely as the sun takes the night.

"Hammett! Put that damn camera down!" Bayne's controlled order shattered the magical illusion.

Wrenching around to face the photographer, Tiana put a small wedge of space between herself and Bayne. As his hold slackened, her body was freed from the exquisite pressure of his, but her mind stubbornly retained the sensation of his penetrating nearness.

"Hammett!" Bayne warned a final time and this time was successful in quieting the camera's insistent whispers.

With a sheepish grin and an apologetic look, Peter lowered his camera. "You're okay, aren't you, Tiana?"

"I'm fine." But her voice wavered, negating her bold statement. Her teeth clamped her lower lip to halt its treacherous trembling. "But if it's all right with you, Peter, I'd like to call it a day."

When Peter started to object, Bayne interjected, "I'll run you home on my way out of the city." One arm had remained circling her back; however, as he spoke, it too was taken from her. "Go ahead and change into your street clothes."

Although Peter's eyebrows flexed, he could not have been any more surprised at Bayne's considerate offer than Tiana was herself. The words of refusal her mind formed were buried beneath a marauding tide of feeling that was carrying away her diminishing willpower with each passing second. The concern in Bayne's eyes captured her, pleasantly wrapping her in an artificial envelope of safety. Numbly, Tiana nodded her assent and weighted legs took her from the room.

The odd feeling Bayne had generated had not completely vanished when Tiana joined him for the ride to SoHo. He unlocked the passenger door and helped her in before rounding the car to take up the driver's position. With a calibrated flick of his wrist, the car roared to life. While it idled, Bayne glanced over at Tiana, surprising her with a genial smile. One of his fingers unbent from where it rested along the top of the steering wheel to point out a house a short distance from where he had parked his car. "You see that house over there?" At her nod, he continued. "Jimmy Walker, who was once mayor of New York, lived there." Bayne slipped the car in gear and soon was within the flow of traffic. Several more times on the brief trip to SoHo, he pointed out landmarks to her. All in all, the conversation was light, casual, and altogether pleasing. Only when he turned the car into her street did Tiana experience a glimmer of apprehension as she caught Bayne giving her a searching look, one so piercing it seemed to tunnel into her soul.

The steering wheel spun back into its original position as his hand synchronized itself with the motion. His eyes were directed forward again. Nonchalantly, almost too much so, he asked, "Why don't you come to Connecticut with me?"

Tiana's jaw opened in shocked disbelief. She could not credit what she had heard! And yet as she turned to him, some woman's instinct combined with the triple-time hammering of her heart, told her she had heard correctly! There was no mistaking his meaning! She quickly pretended to look out of the window, well aware Bayne expected an answer.

After double-parking the car in front of her apartment building, Bayne turned off the motor. He pivoted in her direction and said with a maddening indifference, "I asked you a question. Are you thinking about an answer?"

Intemperately aware of his eyes on her, Tiana courageously lifted her eyes to his, only to find herself incapable of speech. She was positive he could hear the loud thudding of her heart as it beat against her rib cage. Like a drugged somnambulist, her head moved from side to side.

"Are you saying 'no'?" Bayne asked. The mute laughter in his voice joined the twinkling in his eyes to form a deadly conspiracy against her conviction. "Or are you still deciding whether to come or not?"

"Yes." Dreamily, her answer floated on a sigh.

His mouth quirked on one side, the grooves deepening. "Does this 'yes' mean you are coming with me? Or does it mean you are still deciding about coming?" Amusement played hide-and-seek with his patience with the most disarming results on Tiana's pulse.

Rapidly, Tiana blinked as if awakening from a medieval enchanter's spell. A quick gulp of air and then she rushed on, words tripping over one another in riotous confusion. "No! No! I mean no! The 'yes' only meant I agreed that I was not going with you! You see there was nothing to decide. When I shook my head, it meant I wasn't going with you. You do see that, don't you?"

Bayne's laughter halted her runaway tongue as abruptly as it had been loosened. So riddled were her defenses, Tiana collapsed against the leather seat.

"Why?" His word was winged on a chuckle.

"Why?" Tiana echoed dumbly. Then bridling at his

undisguised enjoyment of her embarrassment, she countered with bravura, "I have other plans."

"A boyfriend?"

"No." And at once she could have died for revealing as much to him.

"Then change your plans and come with me?" he persisted with a calmness more volatile than the invitation itself.

"No!" It had come out too shrill and it took conscious effort to soften her voice. "I have other plans."

"Afraid?" he queried.

The word whispered through her like the wind in the trees, bending her determination, her will, to his. Without meaning it to, a betraying moan escaped her slightly parted lips.

"You needn't be afraid," he told her.

But somehow his reasonable tone did not reassure her. It would have been too easy to allow herself to agree. Her mind and her body were victim to the corruption of his control. "I'm not afraid, Bayne. Don't be ridiculous!" Her voice climbed the spectrum of hysteria. "What is there to fear?"

"Yourself?" By comparison his voice was a gentle ripple of sound.

"Me? Afraid of myself?" Tiana squeaked in priceless disbelief. "Bayne Dahlquist, that is the most foolish thing you have ever said to me!"

His mouth crooked designedly. "Is it?"

"Of course it is!" Her voice was off and going higher again. "Why should I be afraid of myself?"

"Oh no, you don't!" He straightened towards her, one arm placed along the back of the seat and the other positioned on the wheel. "You will have to answer that one for yourself. You are too much of an idealist to mistrust the motives of other people or to deal truthfully with your own. Experience should take care of both problems for you. I think I can wait until then."

The reference to her idealism sent Tiana zooming back to earthbound reality. Deliberately raising her chin, she said, "Then you will have a mighty long wait. I have no intention of changing."

"I wouldn't be so sure of that." It could have sounded like a warning but coming from Bayne's lips, it was a promise teemed with secret musing.

With unseeing eyes, Tiana turned away from his magnetism and wildly felt for the handle of the door. Even now, she was not sure he did not have the ability to change her mind. Her fingers closed over the metal projection with desperate readiness. "Thank you for helping me and for the ride home."

"Is that how you thank your knight-errant?" The sultry suggestiveness of his voice sent her stumbling out of the car.

"Thank you!" she flung back before slamming the door with a greater thrust than was strictly necessary. But not so hard and not so fast as to block out Bayne's increasingly familiar laughter.

Wheeling around, Tiana ran to the steps of her building and up them into the main door. Only after she closed the door behind her, did she stop. Resting a shoulder against the wall, she panted breathlessly. And it was not from physical exertion! Inwardly, she fumed over the perverse effect the man had on her. Him and his hateful sense of humor. Then her ire was turned from Bayne to herself, as Tiana realized she had purposefully stood in the entryway listening for the sound of his car, as it sprang to life. She mentally berated herself for being twelve kinds of a fool. What Bayne thought or what he did could not interest her in the least! Or so she told herself as she slowly mounted the stairs to her floor.

Chapter Four

Despite the horrendous downpouring of rain, the Dahlquist Agency was percolating with life when Tiana arrived on Monday morning. The confrontation with Bayne on Friday had left Tiana with a niggling frustration, so she had spent the greater part of the weekend painting to purge herself of the residual feeling of restlessness. Thankfully, it had been a relatively successful maneuver and she was in an exuberant mood in spite of the wetness outside.

"Good morning!" she called out cheerily to Peter, who was huddled over some papers at his desk.

"Don't get carried away! It's not a particularly good morning," Peter grumpily ridiculed her effervescence as he glanced up at Tiana. "It's raining buckets out there and I've scheduled a meeting to rework the Asgard campaign."

"Oh, I forgot about that," she admitted frankly, as she shook her fawn-colored raincoat. Dewdrops of moisture were scattered before she hung the garment to dry.

"Unfortunately, I couldn't forget about it!" Peter rounded dryly. "You heard Bayne tell me about the new deadline. Well, we don't have any choice but to come up with something viable by the end of this week."

"Is that going to be a problem?" Tiana queried, her brow puckered in concern.

"Your guess is as good as mine," Peter quipped before lowering his head back to his paperwork. "My meeting is in twenty minutes. Why don't you come along? It will give you an idea of some of the problems in an advertising campaign and then you can judge for yourself the level of difficulty involved in reworking the Asgard account."

Tiana accepted his suggestion and during the meeting found Peter's words to be prophetically true. She was subjected to a deluge of information and given insights into the inner workings of the agency. One by one, the representatives from the various departments reacted to Peter's announcement and then with renewed commitment outlined other proposals, always with an eye to the marketing data. Admittedly, Tiana was surprised to see how little concern was expressed over creativity and how much effort was expended in going over marketing strategies and surveys.

When the meeting broke up Peter was the first to leave the conference room. Tiana followed neatly in his wake as he cleared the distance to their shared office. Something in his clipped pace hinted to Tiana to keep all her questions until a future time. After they reached the office, she watched in silence as he packed his attaché case and traveled to the door with a singular purpose.

Peter's hand was on the knob of the door when he stopped in his tracks. "I won't be back until sometime after lunch, maybe not at all. It depends on how things go. Handle what you can and if I'm not back leave a memo on the rest."

After he left, Tiana wondered how she could best spend her time. It didn't take long for the perfect solution to come to her. The office was overdue for reorganization of material and a clearing away of some of the clutter. Many of the items Peter stockpiled in his office could be stored in other places. She enthusiastically set to work and by noon the contours of the office had taken on the simplicity of orderliness. She was satisfied with the morning's work. As she stood surveying the results, the hollow rumble of her stomach suggested it was time for lunch. Not wanting to face the torrent outside, she opted for telephoning the lunch counter in the lobby of the building and having a sandwich and soft drink sent up.

As she waited for the delivery, Tiana tackled the monstrous filing cabinets. She did not want the responsibility for throwing out anything, so she neatly organized the folders, replacing lost tabs and double-checking the order of the files. She had just emptied the contents of one drawer when her lunch arrived. After paying the deliveryman she cleared herself a space between the mountains of folders on her desk and sat down to eat. Her chicken salad on toast was soggy and her soda had become diluted by the melting ice but she paid scant attention to it. She was eager to get back to her self-appointed task. She idly munched on the sandwich as she fingered several of the folders. The label "Asgard" caught her eye and she jiggled the expanding file out of the stack. Tiana had just flipped it open when the forced snapping of the door jerked her head upright. Her concentration was irrevocably toppled and swallowing was an impossibility as she met the droll glint in Bayne's eyes with much less confidence than she would have wished. As an added misery her mouth suddenly went dry and the food cleaved embarrassingly to the roof of it.

"So, this is where you've been hiding out," Bayne

drawled amicably enough before crossing the room. Informally, he hung an arm over the file cabinet she had been in the process of emptying. He continued to smile disconcertingly down at her and the sandwich in her mouth took on the consistency of hardening paste.

Incapable of any speech whatsoever, Tiana forced herself to take a generous gulp of her soft drink. For an hysterical instant she thought she would choke as she swallowed the recalcitrant lump of food. When she regained her language ability, she said a·trifle defensively, "I'm not hiding out! I'm straightening the office."

His mouth twisted wryly as his eyes flicked over the stacks of folders on her desk and lazily skirted the room. Then, and only then, did they return to her. Significantly, his eyes meandered over the slender white column of her neck and the jet cascade of her hair which was flung whimsically over one shoulder. He lifted his gaze to encounter hers and his mouth softened. "Nice, very nice. I'm sure Peter will appreciate it."

Her reeling senses betrayed her. Logic told her Bayne was talking about the work she had accomplished in the office. But some fiendish mischief-maker was jumbling the messages her senses were sending to her brain. The steadily sensual vibration in his voice and the devilish light in his eyes were garbling his spoken words. And yet her nerve endings tingled with such a pronounced response that only the silent message got through. Even her blood turned traitor as it carried the drumming of her heart to every inch of her body. Her tongue moistened her lips.

His eyes lowered to follow the movement of her tongue across the tender flesh of her mouth and his smile faded. Now only a wicked curve held the compelling line as he murmured thickly, "I know I would appreciate it."

The potency, the unshakable certainty and the implication of his expression rocked Tiana to the very core of her soul. Confusion embraced her in slippery arms as she was made the willing prisoner of her attraction to Bayne. Why was this happening? Why was he doing this to her? Bayne was toying with her like a jungle cat would play with its defenseless prey moments before it devoured it. But even that ghastly realization could not save her. Tiana was snared by the magic between them and lost in a world she had never known existed.

His eyes glinted dangerously like crystals of polished green malachite. "If only you weren't such an innocent, you could find out just how appreciative I can be."

Innocent! The word tugged at her heart strings. Again, the hated reminder of how little he thought of her. Would she ever be free of the hurt that partnered his cruel taunts? He played the game by rules that Tiana could never master. However long or hard she tried, Bayne would remain the champion. It was no use! It would never be any different! A jagged abyss separated them more surely than time or experience ever could.

Her brown eyes, freckled in sadness, were averted from him in baleful sorrow. If only she did not care! But she did! And she was only beginning to comprehend how much. Her spirit quelled, Tiana brokenly accused, "You promised not to talk about our differences."

"But I didn't. I only said . . . ah, I see. From your point of view, I guess it could be interpreted that way," he sighed. "Sometimes, fair nymph, I despair of you ever growing up."

The gentle regret in his voice turned her gaze back to him but she was at once sorry. His voice might have been infinitely compassionate but the amusement in his eyes as they flirted with her was nothing short of mockery; cold, clear, unrelenting mockery.

Bayne shook his head for no discernible reason and his eyes closed for one brief instant. When they opened his face was again the mask of a competent and noticeably complacent business executive, refuting all that had recently passed between them. "By the way, where is Peter?"

The mention of Peter's name jolted Tiana back from the utopian country of her secret musings. "He went out to a client meeting. He wasn't sure if he would be back this afternoon. May I give him a message from you?"

"Only that I'll see him tomorrow." Bayne crossed to the door and opened it. "And Tiana, I did miss you this weekend."

Surprise opened her mouth and flaring annoyance closed it. His parting shot about her refusal to accompany him to Connecticut flooded her with conflicting emotions. She had thought all her frustration had been worked out of her system by painting, but now she knew that Bayne could bring it all back again. Drat, Bayne Dahlquist anyway! Tiana balled up her sandwich wrapper and paper bag and in a fury of misspent anger threw it away. She had pushed Bayne from her mind once and she could do it again!

Grabbing the Asgard file from her desk, Tiana began to read over the contents. From all indications, it held previous campaign information as well as several ideas that had initially been considered for the current one. One of the tentative concepts caught her attention and Tiana found herself returning to it time and again.

Finally when she gave up hope of defeating her interest in it, she reached for her sketching pad.

The afternoon spun away into the limitless void of the past as she diligently worked over her tablet. At last, when all her creative impulses had been pinned on paper, she lowered the drawing pad. Only then did Tiana notice the increased sound of traffic in the corridor. Quitting time was upon her and she had not even finished cleaning out one drawer, much less the whole cabinet. She got a fresh storage envelope for her sketches and after labeling it, placed them in her desk for safekeeping. With a rising sense of duty, Tiana decided to stay overtime and at least finish the job she had started on the one filing cabinet.

The building gradually quieted as more and more people joined the exodus. She worked for some time until she had finished all but one drawer. She was replacing the folders in the fourth drawer when the door burst open, smacking the wall as Peter literally bounded into the room.

Swinging his attaché case into the air, Peter sent it skidding across the top of his desk. He vaulted across the room and pulled her upright by her hands from where she had been crouched before the metal cabinet. "I can't believe I caught you in! It saves me a trip to your apartment." Peter danced her around the room in ever dizzying circles. Faster and faster he whirled her, until her feet were lifted above the floor.

Unable to tolerate any more, she was forced to beg, "Peter, please put me down! Please!"

"Tiana! Tiana! Tiana!" The mantra of her name evoked a further elevation of his spirit, a feat that Tiana would have previously considered impossible.

"Peter, what happened?" She laughed, catching his excitement and making it her own.

"I don't know where to start!" His eyes shone with a maniacal light that torched her face with unrestrained glee.

"The beginning is always a good place to start," she prompted.

Meaninglessly Peter asked, "Was it the first time I looked up to see you standing so nervously in my office? Or was it later when I saw those first pictures of you come to life in my darkroom?"

"What do I have to do with this?" Alarmed, Tiana croaked in a threadbare voice.

"Everything! Something! A little! A lot!" he cried, his uncontrollable jubilation had evidently not run its full course. "Who knows what unique combination is necessary for all the parts to come together in one masterpiece?"

Tiana's brow webbed as she seriously began to question Peter's sanity. He was ranting and raving like a madman. "What on earth are you talking about, Peter?" She tried to imitate the tone she had heard mothers use with irascible children.

She must have had some success for she saw the wild euphoria dim fractionally as his eyes focused on her earnest face. Slipping a brotherly arm around her shoulders, he said, "I think you had better sit down for this one."

Obediently, Tiana sat down, but all the while she thought it was Peter who actually needed to be sitting. She was more than pleased to see him swish aside a stack of papers from the corner of his desk and prop his frame on it. Calm and reasonable! At all costs she must remain calm and reasonable! If she was, perhaps some of it would rub off on him.

Peter took a great swallow of air and blew it out in a whistling funnel. "You must think I have flipped my lid!"

Calm and reasonable, she told herself for the third time. Don't let him suspect how close to the mark he is. Tiana primly folded her hands on her lap, a pristine gesture to disguise her insidious curiosity. "Suppose you tell me your news."

Peter drew a long, replenishing breath. "There was no use in telling you before because it was such a long shot. And when I say long shot, you better believe I mean it! But we made it and that's what counts."

"We?" The word stuck in her throat like a fuzzy ball of cotton. And then a suspicion began to unwind within her. It had no name as yet but Tiana had the altogether distinct impression that she would not be quite as thrilled as Peter when she heard about it. *We?* There should have been no we about it! By all rights Peter should have said *I*.

"Yes! We!" Peter exclaimed. "You remember meeting the Averys at Starke's opening. Well, what you may or may not know, is that they have been looking for a model for a new fragrance they are putting out soon."

A vague memory began to materialize but before Tiana could get a firm handle on it, Peter resumed his exuberant talking.

"They need a fresh model, someone not known to the public, who is contractually free to sign an exclusive contract. You are the type they are looking for and after seeing the pictures I took of you Friday, you are the one they want!"

Vacant brown eyes stared at Peter, unable or unwilling to comprehend what he was telling her.

Reading her bewildered expression, Peter charged excitedly, "Don't you understand what I'm saying? It means, you now have the most coveted cosmetic contract of the year! It's right in your hip pocket! It's a one-year exclusive with a three-year renewable option."

Her jaw dropped in shock and implausibility. "Peter, you can't be serious!"

"I can! I am!"

"But, Peter, I'm not a model. I don't even want to be a model. Whatever made you think I would be interested in a contract?"

Peter's lean fingers hooked over the edge of the desk as he bent forward. "Don't you know what this means?"

Her eyes widened in a pliant tolerance more eloquent than any words.

"Listen, hon, with the right investments you could get a base income for life. And if they pick up your option, you could be another Catherine Hunter. I'm talking a six figure contract!" Having shared his golden nugget of information, Peter was content to relax, crossing his arms in front of his chest as he waited for it to sink in.

"I don't know anything about modeling. This is a vastly different proposition than posing for a few pictures for you," she reminded him.

Now it was Peter who exhibited the flexible tolerance. "We know that! It's all been taken into consideration. I spent the entire afternoon going over your pictures with the Averys. There is enough promise in those pictures to justify giving you the contract."

"I just couldn't do it!" she said flatly.

Peter pushed aside her reluctance. "Not to worry! Tomorrow you will sign with the Williams Modeling Agency. They handle Catherine. If you want to go with another firm you can. But they are the best and have a very solid reputation. Since you will be coming to them with a major contract, I feel sure they will bend over backwards to accommodate you." Peter smiled.

"Didn't you hear what I said? I don't want to model." Exasperation touched off a panic in her voice as she tried to convince him.

"Just relax, Tiana." Peter's hand chopped the air. "I know this is all very sudden and probably unexpected. But believe me, a chance like this only comes along once in a lifetime. Trust me!"

"I don't know. I need time to think," she confessed soberly.

"If it were up to me, you would have all the time in the world. Unfortunately, I simply don't have it to give you. We have been looking for the right model for some time now. The Averys are extremely anxious to get the campaign under way. George is supposed to retire as soon as the new line is launched and his health is not good. Also, the longer a product is in planning the greater the chance of industrial espionage. This line has got to get out soon!"

"Since I need time to think and you can't give it to me, maybe you should find someone else," proffered Tiana softly.

"You haven't been listening! I told you, we don't have anyone else we can use. Don't you think we would have already signed them if we did?" Impatience drew a hard line down the center of his words.

Duly chastised, Tiana mouthed a penitent, "Oh!"

"I suppose we could sacrifice the Avery account," Peter commented to no one in particular.

"You mean give up the advertising account?" Fright edged its way into her voice.

"We may not have any choice." Mercilessly, Peter had administered the killing stroke; a Toledan sword cutting through her resistance with all the effort of tempered steel slicing thin air.

"Are you saying that if I don't sign this modeling contract, the Dahlquist Agency will lose the Avery contract?" He couldn't mean it! Surely someone else could be found to do the ad, someone with more experience, more desire to model. There must be someone, somewhere who could do the job!

"Come on, Tiana! You know how competitive advertising is in New York. The Avery account was Bayne's first, but sentimentality never put food on the table. If we can't deliver what they want, there is nothing to stop them from going to an agency that can and will." The calibrated silence following his announcement was more sinister, more insidious than anything he had said.

An icy finger of misgiving traced a shivery groove down the middle of her back. And Tiana fought the twin demons of doubt and guilt; doubting she could actually perform as a professional model and intense guilt about letting down everyone if she adamantly refused to try. The death toll of silence reverberated with torturous significance until Tiana thought she would crack under the stress of it. Peter seemed so confident of her ability, a confidence she did not share.

Peter's eyes held her face and an analytical gleam took note of her expression. "Since it is an exclusive contract, you couldn't take up any other modeling assignments without renegotiating. And since you will only be representing one product, you should have a lot of time even after the public appearances are subtracted out. I can arrange for you to be granted a leave of absence as my assistant and you can come back whenever you like, possibly in a position as a staff artist. Or if you want to freelance with your art, I could put you in contact with some of the right people."

The proverbial carrot, dangling just out of reach. "Peter, you know I want to be a commercial artist more than anything in the world."

"Good! Then it's settled!" Peter concluded.

He was moving too fast for Tiana and she balked. "But what if I don't want to take the leave? What if I want to stay right here as your assistant and take my chances on working my way up to a staff position?"

"If you don't sign the modeling contract and we lose the Avery account because of it, I seriously doubt there will be much chance of you moving up. Avery is one of our larger accounts. I feel sure budget tightening would follow if we were to lose it." He put the onus on her, saddling Tiana with the financial future of the agency.

"Peter, could I lose my job?" Fear darkened her eyes.

"You know what they say, last hired, first fired." He shrugged negligently.

"And if I model for the Avery account, I could still keep my job here?" An alternative had been snatched from her when Peter had imperiled her job. The question was merely a formality.

"Yep!"

She sighed. Defeat now veiled her shadowed eyes. "All right. You win. I just hope you know what you're doing."

"Trust me!" Peter clapped his hands together, relishing his victory. "Come on, I'll take you to dinner! It's the least I can do and it will give me a chance to outline what you need to know."

The angle of her head spanned weariness and reluctance. But in the end, Tiana agreed to dinner and in doing so validated Peter's chancy plan for her future.

Truly spoken, Peter did diagram what Tiana would be doing over the next few days. It sounded so simple when he listed her appointments. However, during the roll call of days that followed, Tiana discovered, to her horror, that their conversation had given her no real perception of how busy she would be. Her time ceased belonging to her and became instead the possession of countless others.

The very next day, Tiana signed with the Williams Modeling Agency. A Mrs. Clark, now her agent, pirated her to an all-day session at one of the city's exclusive beauty spas for a complete make-over. By the time she left there, Tiana had received lessons in using a satchel of beauty products she had been given, but that was only after she had endured every conceivable beauty enhancing procedure ever devised. All things considered, the procedures were bearable and a few, by their own novelty, interesting. One though caused her more that a moment's pause. She submitted to having her long fall of hair cut. "Styled" was the word they used! But it was too late to protest when more than eight inches in length was sheered with the first snip of the scissors. She swallowed down her budding grief and could only pray that the hair stylist knew what he was doing. More and more of her hair joined the growing pile on the floor as her entire appearance was radically altered. When he was done, Tiana was left with a shiny ebony cap of hair, which, when blown dry, formed tiny, wispy points that scarcely covered the top of her ears.

She could hardly believe it. With her shorn hair she looked exactly like a sexless ten-year-old child instead of the model destined to be the next Catherine Hunter. It certainly was a change, to put it mildly. Her eyes, never small, now appeared as giant saucers suspended above the high ridge of her cheekbones. She wondered what the Averys would say when they saw what had been done to her in the name of beauty. Perhaps now they would be forced to find another model. That thought, if no other, brightened her outlook.

Chapter Five

Although Tiana spent a goodly portion of the last forty-eight hours attending to tasks connected with modeling, she had not actually signed her contract. That formality would be taken care of today at the law office of Barrington, Kissane and Thrombley, counselors for the Williams Modeling Agency.

In only two days, the transformation in Tiana's appearance was amazing. Subtle changes had produced a girl looking vastly different from the one who existed only days ago. Dressed in a designer dress and short matching jacket in shades of misty plum, Tiana could have passed for any young woman born to the silver spoon, instead of the nervous and anxious one she actually was. Things were happening too soon and too fast for Tiana to maintain any degree of equilibrium. Everything was out of kilter, like a tipsy carousel going round and round, turning crazily. And she could not get off.

Upon entering the attorney's office, Tiana could not conceal her stunned surprise at the abundant number of people present. For one reason or another, she had expected only her lawyer. Obviously, this was not the case! Mr. Avery, Mr. Thrombley, Peter and another gentleman rose to their feet. And Bayne! He was there too! And Martha Avery was seated on the couch.

The next few minutes were nothing less than a disjointed segment juxtaposed in a bizarre choreography of faces, introductions, and handshakes. Tiana had the preposterous feeling of being an unwilling actress in a scene written for the stage. Bravely, she tried to rearrange her expression to hide the inner turmoil which lay so readily below the surface. Her ability was sorely tested as Bayne took her hand in his much larger one and smiled down at her with eyes as opaque as green slate. She might have pondered his presence or its possible ramifications if she had not been so acutely aware of him. When he actually touched her she could have sworn her hand tingled warmly for some uncounted minutes afterward.

Still musing over the odd sense of breathlessness that had accompanied Bayne's handshake, Tiana was ushered to a chair behind the desk. Several documents were fanned out for her signature. A gold pen was produced as if by a magician's slight of hand.

"Should I read all this?" Tiana asked no one in particular.

Obligingly, Mr. Thrombley, her attorney, answered, "There is no need to read it. I can give you every assurance that it has been well scrutinized. Except for the attached rider, it is a standard model's contract." He bestowed upon her a professional smile designed to reassure without yielding a personal commitment.

The slender pen in Tiana's fingers weighed heavily. She glanced down at her moist prints on the burnished patina and wondered at her own timidity. She rebuked herself for allowing her fears to have such a free rein with her spirit. Catching her breath she looked to Mr. Thrombley for guidance.

He was still smiling although it was fainter. With a

stiffened index finger he tapped several lined spaces on the contracts. "You sign here, here, and here."

With whitened fingertips pressed compactly to the pen, she put her name on the papers before her. She had no sooner finished the last one, than the documents were speedily whisked away and handed to a waiting secretary. And then what happened next was mingled forever with surprise and confusion in her memory.

As if a dam had burst, good will and best wishes poured forth from every corner of the room! The lawyer shook her hand, pumping it with lusty effort. Peter gave her a squeeze across the shoulders that passed for a hug. George and Martha Avery each kissed her on the cheek, much like a favorite aunt and uncle might. Bayne, whether planned or accidental, was the last to offer Tiana his congratulations.

At his approach, Tiana froze. The smile on her lips was immovable as he stepped closer. The earlier contact of his flesh with hers during the handshake, made Tiana intensely aware of him and of her reaction to him. He hesitated but a second before placing his hands on her shoulders, his fingers gently cupping the sloping incline. She sensed the chiding mockery beneath the firm line of his mouth even as his hands drew her to him.

"Let me add my best wishes for a successful campaign, Tiana." The seductive timbre of his voice deepened fractionally and tremors of awareness were sent coursing through her.

Automatically, Tiana raised her head, her eyes intently fastened on the cynical curve of his mouth. Her own lips parted in unconscious anticipation, teased with possibility. Her eyelids closed for an instant as his auburn head moved nearer. Every muscle and cell in her body was tensed, craving the act that would bring release.

His warmed breath caressed her cheek the instant before his lips touched it. It was over quickly. And as Bayne's arms extended her back to her original position, Tiana was not quite sure what had happened. Her eyes opened slowly, reluctantly. As if to do so any faster would drive the fleeting dream from her senses. The room still buzzed with conversation and talk, none of it intruding in Tiana's thoughts. She knew only one thing. Her awareness of Bayne had grown into an almost pain in the pit of her stomach.

Bayne smiled then, one of his rare movements that lifted his lips and lit a fire behind his eyes. He was unduly disarming and Tiana could feel the acceleration of her pulse. She was sure no one else in the office saw him lift one brow in silent question. It was a demand made of her and she gladly complied. Her smile caught the flame of his, kindling something very secret and private between them.

It was almost with annoyance that Tiana accepted the cup of coffee the secretary was handing her. It meant her gaze broke from Bayne's and it cost her a curious feeling of loss. As Tiana ladled a teaspoon of sugar into her cup, Mrs. Avery beckoned her.

"Why don't you come over here?" The older woman patted the cushion next to her on the couch where she had repositioned herself.

Tiana's dark lashes fluttered as she turned to Bayne. The amusement in his expression decided the issue for her. Glad to be out of the limelight and away from his glinting gaze, Tiana joined Mrs. Avery. As if by a mutually unvoiced decision, the men pooled together on the other side of the office.

Mrs. Avery, her blue eyes twinkling, said, "You must be very excited with so much happening in the last few days. Peter told me you had no idea you were actually being considered until the decision was made."

"It's true!" Tiana took a tentative sip of her coffee, forestalling any elaboration.

The other woman made a sound that passed for a chuckle. "I can sympathize! It must be very new and strange to you. I'm sorry we had to cloak everything in such secrecy. But now that you are under contract to us, there is no reason why you can't be told the details."

"I wish you would tell me," Tiana admitted. She was likely to get more information from Mrs. Avery than from either Bayne or Peter.

Martha Avery, her eyes fluidly sliding to Tiana as she leaned forward, said, "I imagine you have some inkling of the type of image we want you to project simply from the way your hair was done."

At the mere mention of her short hair, Tiana's hand mechanically ran feeling fingers over the shortened length. "When I first saw it, I thought they had made an awful mistake. It makes me look about ten years old."

"Not ten years old, my dear," Martha corrected. "What we had in mind was an ageless quality, an eternally youthful creature, the part of a woman that is always young and vulnerable."

"Oh," Tiana said in a tiny voice.

"Now for the best news of all!" Martha confided. "You know this is the last campaign before my husband retires." She paused to allow Tiana to nod. Then she continued, "Well, because it is the last, we have planned a very special product. We had a wonderful fragrance developed. It is a light woodsy blend with just a touch of floral. It really is an appealing scent and marketing research indicates the time is right for it. Women by the droves are returning to softer, less strident cosmetics. This line, this fragrance is called "Elfin Magic." And you, dear, will become known to all as "The Elf!"

The Elf! Tiana's mind silently shrieked. Subconsciously, she had characterized the Avery model as someone sleek and sophisticated, not unlike Catherine Hunter. And she had felt more than a little giddy at the prospect of being classified in such enviable company. She should have realized that it was an impossibility from the start. With her gamine face and hair she could not even approach the word *glamor* much less serve as an example of it. As it was now, nothing was left to Tiana but to gather the store of her willpower and prevent her face from showing the shock hedged disappointment. "Elfin Magic?" She experimented with the sound on her tongue.

Then a depressing thought triggered her fertile imagination. Bayne knew about the new fragrance line! Of course he did! He was searching for someone to act the part of an elf when he goaded her without mercy about her innocence and idealism. Bayne thought of her as an elfin creature or he would have never let her get the contract. Her mind's jeering eye recalled elves as sexless creatures, untouched by the real world. They frolicked with abandon in meadows, streams, and woodland. Is that how Bayne really thought of her? Was the sparkle in his eyes when he congratulated her put there by amusement over her situation? Her eyes skittered across the room to the man she considered a giant among equals.

His eyes met hers as if by prearrangement. The diagonal tightrope between them scintillated with ungrounded promise. But the stark meaning of his gaze was not known to Tiana. Was this yet another device of his to mock her? Defenseless against the vibrancy in his stare, Tiana tore her eyes from him to settle safely on Martha Avery.

Noticing nothing of Tiana's momentary distraction, Martha continued her explanation, "So you see, the concept of Elfin Magic was not a whim or a lucky guess. Oh no! We planned it for years! Even though the formula is only about two years old, we have had the name in mind for a good deal longer. The name Elfin Magic holds a special significance for us. Our family name of Avery means protector of elves. It comes from the Old English and originally meant descendant of Aelfric. Once we decided on using the Elfin concept, it was a hop, skip and a jump to the magic. After all, love is magic, as every woman who has ever been in love knows. Can you imagine a better name for our last fragrance line than Elfin Magic?"

"No. It sounds perfect! I wish you and your husband every success!" Tiana meant it, despite her own blighted hope of having Bayne ever see her in a different light.

"Thank you, Tiana," Martha replied earnestly. "By the way, what do you think of the rider attached to your contract? I don't mind telling you, it took some doing! Oh, not that we didn't want you to have every consideration. But we almost gave up on finding something agreeable in only two days. However, Bayne was bound and determined to have it written in as part of your contract. So nothing would do but to get it for him."

A warning gong was struck. Concentric circles of alarm were sent vibrating through Tiana at the mention of Bayne's name. "I haven't seen the rider. What were the terms of it?" she asked softly, casually, consequently belying the cantankerous thumping of her heart.

"There were several minor points but the one causing the problem was getting you the apartment. But bless his heart, Bayne worked it all out."

"Did he?" A sense of volcanic hysteria underscored her voice as Tiana forced a saccharine smile to her lips.

Bayne! She did not want him interfering in her life the way he invaded her peace of mind.

"Oh my, yes!" Martha swished her hand through the air as if to dispell any doubts lingering there. "Bayne worked it out with Catherine. He was so smart to think of her. You see, she has one of our apartments on Fifth Avenue as long as she is under contract to us. Now with Catherine talking about retiring when her current contract expires, the apartment would have become available then. But Bayne would simply not wait. So he talked with Catherine about the two of you rooming together until her contract is up. It was an excellent idea. And as Bayne pointed out, Catherine can be a big help to you."

"But I already have an apartment!" Surprise and more than a tinge of anger raised the decibel level of Tiana's voice so that every pair of eyes in the room swung to her. Embarrassed at calling attention to herself, she deliberately lowered it. "I have an apartment in SoHo. I'm subleasing it and I just couldn't let it go. It was nice of you to include the other one in the contract but I'm afraid I won't be using it." Tiana almost bit back the words when she saw the baffled look on Martha's face. "Please, don't be . . ."

"I beg to differ." Bayne's clipped words sliced off the end of her statement. He stood next to Tiana. Without her observing him, Bayne had detached himself from the other group and took up a position flanking the couch. "The apartment on Fifth Avenue was included for very sound reasons. There is no question about it. You will take up residence there."

If Bayne had ever been insufferable in the past, it was nothing compared to his domineering, patronizing arrogance now. Vigorously, Tiana shook her head. Tiny black feathers of hair tickled the upper edges of her cheek bones, but she was numb to the sensation.

Determination shimmered in her eyes like splintery points of smoked topaz. A hush fell over the room as all attention was focused on Tiana and her formidable opponent.

Undaunted, Tiana picked her words with the greatest care. "I do appreciate everything you've done, Mr. Dahlquist, but it would be both impractical and inconvenient for me to move."

"And since when have you decided to become practical?" Bayne challenged critically. Fractures of burning green fire circled the diamond-hard pupils of his eyes; pupils contracted to pinpoints of Stygian blackness.

She grappled with an upheaval of fright. She drew in a soundless breath, only too aware of the untamed savagery in his gaze. Swiftly, she amended, "I can't break my lease. It is up in five months or so, perhaps we can talk about it then. That way Catherine would not have to share her apartment. I might be able to take it over when she moves out."

Bayne answered her suggestion by arching one eyebrow, throwing the faded scar into vivid relief. "No, Miss Spencer, you will not move five months from now or even in one month. You will move in with Catherine by the end of this week. It has already been arranged."

"Not by me, it hasn't!" she said furiously, rage encroaching on her control. The silence following her outburst deepened until Tiana felt it like a damp mist swirling around her.

Inescapably, Tiana was forced to acknowledge the smoldering solidarity of his will or risk the costliest of put-downs. But she had no intention of permitting him to control the fabric of her life like he already did the individual threads of her emotion. No! She refused him any more power than he already owned. But by the same token, she could not afford to push him into open

warfare in front of others. There was no doubt in her
mind who the loser would be in such a confrontation.
Carefully tempering her voice, she added, "Maybe we
can discuss it later. I'm sure we can come to some
agreement."

With a deceptive silkiness, he rejoined, "We can
come to an agreement right now. You will move in
tomorrow or the day after at the latest."

"I told you . . ."

Her response to his despotic order was stopped cold
by a deflecting motion of his hand. Although he made
no physical attempt to touch her, the words were
stopped in her throat as if his strong hands were
choking her breath. She gasped as much from the
abruptly curtailed anger as from the unmistakable
message being reflected from the mirrors of his eyes.

"There is not one logical or practical reason why you
cannot be in that apartment by the end of this week. If
you think you might have one, I will listen to it now."
Each word was cast in a granite mold, hard and
immovable.

"I . . . I want to keep the apartment in SoHo. I feel
a personal obligation to do so." Her voice trembled
weakly on the brink of total dissolution.

"You can keep it as a studio if you wish. But you will
live at the Fifth Avenue address." Bayne had yielded
nothing.

"I don't want to crowd Catherine or take away her
privacy." Her tone heartened at the prospect of
submitting a logical reason, especially under the circumstances. Bayne had a decided dictatorial streak in
him.

Bayne, however, was not impressed. His face remained inscrutable. "Nonsense! Catherine travels a
good deal and anyway the apartment is certainly large
enough for the two of you."

Tiana, hell-bent on making another stand, surveyed the others in the office. But she found no sympathy, no understanding of her plight. All she saw was undisguised interest in the outcome and one or two sly smiles, no doubt over the projected winner. As a last resort, Tiana turned to Martha Avery. Disappointment fell hard. For although the older woman looked at her with empathy she made no effort to become her ally.

"Tomorrow?" Bayne lassoed Tiana's questing eyes.

"I couldn't possibly before Friday," Tiana answered without thinking.

The slow indemnity of Bayne's grin told her even before the collective expulsion of breaths, that she had surrendered to his will. In effect, she had agreed to move in by the end of the week, which was precisely what he had wanted her to do. For one crazed moment Tiana almost retracted her agreement. But then someone, she thought it was Peter, said how productive it was for an artist to have a separate studio. And then someone else spoke up telling her how nice Catherine was and what a wonderful roommate she would make. It sounded like something Mrs. Avery would say but Tiana thought it might have been George who said it. And soon, Tiana even forgot why she objected to the move in the first place.

Perhaps Martha summed it up best. "We, all of us here, have your best interests at heart. You are inexperienced and Catherine will be an invaluable guide to you, and living on Fifth Avenue, we won't have to be quite so concerned over your physical safety. It would be an inverted form of snobbery, not to make the move. As you become known to the public, you will undoubtedly welcome what little privacy we can provide for you."

Tiana had to admit there was some validity to what was being said. If only it had been put to her this way from the start instead of Bayne ordering her to comply with the arrangement. A situation that was not of her making but his. It still rankled! She didn't know why he had done it, but knowing how his mind worked, she felt sure it was for some pragmatic reason of his own devising, probably wholly concerned with business.

Chapter Six

Tiana was allotted Friday free except for a session scheduled with the costuming tailor. She used the remainder of the day to pack her belongings for the move to the new apartment. When all was said and done, she took with her only the two suitcases of clothes she had originally brought with her to New York. She left her books and painting equipment in SoHo. The idea of keeping the efficiency as a studio had taken root and Tiana was anticipating the joy of having her own separate studio.

Early Friday evening, a cab took her to the address on Fifth Avenue. It was a magnificent building, one of those staid citadels of exclusiveness keynoting the lifestyle of the highest strata of society. As the taxi pulled up to the front of the somber building a uniformed doorman hastened to help her and to collect her luggage.

Tiana stood for a moment on the sidewalk. Here, more than any other place on the island, a prevailing sense of the city swept through her. Here was glamour and tradition! Now for the first time Tiana realized how fortunate she was. From where she stood, Tiana could see a stretch of large apartment buildings extending northward as far as she could see. In the opposite direction was the edge of one of the world's most opulent shopping districts and across the avenue was Central Park, quilted with its variegated greenery at its peak. Tiana, aware that the doorman was awaiting her, stepped into the lobby of the building. It was like a dream come true.

Catherine Hunter answered the door with all the warmth and sincerity of their initial meeting. The redhead was dressed casually in lavender slacks and an ecru silk blouse. Her clothes did not in any way diminish her beauty while adding a cover of easy intimacy. "Would you like to see the apartment or would you rather relax with some coffee?" Catherine inquired pleasantly as she led Tiana through the marble-floored foyer into the living room.

"Oh, I'd rather see it!" Tiana answered enthusiastically as her widening brown eyes took in the vastness of the living room. Two long couches and several occasional chairs as well as a number of glass-topped tables did not lessen the ocean of space before her. A collection of decorative mirrors spread along one wall and picture windows along another furthered the illusion of openness. Nothing but carefully blended shades of off-white and beige met her eye. Everywhere Tiana looked there was gleam and cream, almost too perfect.

As if reading her mind, Catherine laughed. "I know! It looks like it should be photographed for a magazine! Periodically, Martha and George replace the furnishings. It's all done by an interior decorator. So I'm sure if you don't like your bedroom, they will be glad to have it done over for you. Come along and I'll show it to you."

They crossed the buff-colored carpeting of the living room and entered a hallway. Tiana found her bedroom was done in magnificent shades of blue, which instantly appealed to her artist's feel for color. The double bed was covered in a floral patterned spread of plush quilting which matched the drapes. Natural bamboo accessories lightened the overall effect without cloying the senses.

"It's perfect! I wouldn't change a thing!" Tiana declared.

"Sure?" Catherine questioned.

"Absolutely!"

Catherine smiled and led the way to the next room. It was apparently a spare bedroom converted to a den-office. The furniture was less formal and there was a desk for working and a television set. At the end of the hall was Catherine's bedroom. It was decorated in kinetic hues of lime green and was complemented by white wicker.

As they made their way to the compact kitchen they traveled through the dining room. Once in the kitchen, Catherine asked, "How about that coffee now?"

Tiana nodded her agreement, and Catherine started brewing coffee. "I want you to know, I'm really happy you've moved in with me," Catherine volunteered. "Except for entertaining, this place is too large for one person. As it is, I'm gone about half of the time."

"I feel so much better about the move knowing that," Tiana confessed, obviously relieved that Catherine did not consider her an intruder. "I was afraid I was forced on you."

Musical laughter met Tiana's fear. "On the contrary! Even before Bayne mentioned you getting the Elfin Magic contract, I was thinking about getting a roommate." Her emerald eyes shimmered with undisguised enjoyment. "I think you were the only one with any objections. Peter and Martha both told me about your reluctance and how Bayne bullied you into agreeing.

Someone should have warned you not to attempt to oppose him. Bayne usually gets his way."

"I wasn't sure . . ." The end of Tiana's remark was lost in the sound of the door chime.

"I'll get the door, if you'll finish the tray," Catherine said. "Bring it to the living room when you're ready."

Tiana placed the service on the tray and was just positioning it on a low table in the living room when Catherine entered from the foyer. She was carrying Tiana's two suitcases.

When Tiana made a move to help her, Catherine shook her head. "I'll put them over here until after we have our coffee." She put the bags down next to the wall and joined Tiana on one of the off-white velvet couches. She slipped her flat shoes off and curled her long legs under her body. "Make yourself comfortable, Tiana. It's your home too."

Tiana smiled but kept her feet firmly planted on the floor. She appreciated the warmth of the other woman but something nettled her. With a sense of pique, Tiana realized Bayne had engineered this move for the convenience of his girlfriend. It had nothing to do with helping Tiana in any way.

"The building man said that you only had two cases. Are you having your other things sent over later?" Catherine asked before sipping her black coffee.

"That's all I'm bringing. I'm keeping the other apartment as a studio. I left everything else there, at least until my lease is up, which won't be for several more months."

Catherine chuckled. "You just relieved me of my one concern. I would be ashamed to show you all the clothes I have packed away in every spare corner of this place, not to mention the seasonal changes I keep in storage at the cleaners. It was all I could do to get my stuff out of the closet in the bedroom. I had a nightmare of you arriving with trunks and boxes of clothes and nowhere to put them."

Tiana laughed. "Don't worry about closet space on my account! In fact, you can have back some of the space in my closet if you'd like."

"I would like! But within a very short time you will be facing the same space problem I have. Don't sit there and shake your head!" Catherine said with a grin. "Believe me, inside of one month you will have more clothes than you ever thought about owning at one time. You will be making many appearances at quasi-business affairs and each one will require something different because you will never know when a photographer will snap a picture or what people you will be meeting again. However, it's not as bad as it sounds. One of the fringe benefits of modeling is we usually get things wholesale and sometimes gratis as a walking advertisement for a store or designer. Either way, you will probably get a liberal clothing allowance. The Averys are very good about taking care of their own."

Sighing deeply, Tiana said, "It all seems so strange! I never planned on being a model and sometimes I think it has all been an awful mistake."

"We all feel like that at times," Catherine assured her. "Didn't you want to be an artist?"

"I still do. Peter got me temporarily side-tracked with this modeling contract. I really don't understand how it all happened. One minute I was sitting there sketching and the next . . ." Tiana gasped, shutting her eyes against the unwanted memory. Now she remembered what it was she had been sketching! In all the excitement Tiana had left the Asgard drawings in her desk. Here it was the end of the week and no one had seen her work.

"Is something wrong?" Concern ringed Catherine's question.

Tiana opened her eyes to see the redhead tensely leaning forward. Hastily, she sought to ease Catherine's evident distress. "No. No. I just remembered something I forgot to do." And as the other woman shot her a silent look of inquiry, Tiana explained. "The day Peter told me about the Elfin Magic account I had been working on some sketches for another client. We had a one-week deadline. Well, I didn't think Peter would be coming back to the office so I put them in my desk drawer. In all the furor this week, I forgot to tell him about it and today was the last day."

With a thoughtful gleam in her eyes, Catherine asked, "If Monday is too late, why not give Peter a call right now?" She did not wait for Tiana to answer but uncoiled from her position and went to the telephone.

"It won't do any good because he would have to see them in order to judge."

"I'll call Peter anyway and see what he wants to do. He can always drop by the office to have a look at them." Catherine lifted the receiver and began to punch the tiny buttons on the dial plate. After a few moments, she said, "This is Catherine Hunter. Please call me back." Then glancing at Tiana she explained, "He is out so I left the message on his answering machine."

"Well, thank you for trying but it really isn't urgent. Peter probably wouldn't want to use them anyway," Tiana commented.

With the telephone receiver still in her hand, Catherine said, "I want to try one more thing."

Tiana watched with budding curiosity as Catherine called another number. Surprise jolted her when she heard the redhead mention the name Mr. Dahlquist.

Bayne! She was calling Bayne! But then as Tiana heard Catherine give a message similar to the one she left for Peter, she calmed down. Apparently Bayne was not home either.

Replacing the receiver, Catherine returned to her place on the couch. "As you probably heard, I left a message with Bayne's service. But he may have already left town for the weekend. I'm sorry I couldn't have been more helpful."

"Oh Catherine, you did everything you could," Tiana hurriedly said. "It's not important anyway."

"More coffee?" Catherine asked as she poured more into her cup. As Tiana shook her head in refusal, the green-eyed woman settled back into her former position, legs tucked under her. "Still, there must be something we could do."

"I can't imagine what it would be. Besides, there is a chance the work was already sent over. If not, then we can try on Monday morning," Tiana said.

"If they sent it over today, Monday will be too late." Catherine drew a thoughtful sip from her cup. Then putting the cup in its saucer, she placed them both on the table. Alertly she sat up, her forefinger jabbing the air. "There is something we can do. We can go to the agency, get the drawings and send them over to the client ourselves."

"We can't do that!" Tiana was horrified.

"Why not?"

"What if the other ideas haven't been sent over?" Tiana offered the first reason coming to mind.

Shrugging, Catherine replied, "We'll check around the office and see if we can find them. If we can't let's take a chance and send yours over. If we find them, then we can afford to wait until Monday to show them to Peter. They are just sending over ideas. They're not making a presentation are they?"

"No. But I still couldn't do it without someone approving them first."

Crossing her arms in front of her chest, Catherine's slender fingers drummed a silent message. "Bayne may be out of town and heaven knows when we'll catch up with Peter. I think we should take a chance and do it. You don't have anything to lose. And who knows, you might have something to gain."

It all sounded so acceptable, so reasonable, when Catherine argued the point. But Tiana had no trouble reminding herself that at its best, it was a demented suggestion, full of undreamt dangers. "I don't think so."

"Naturally, I haven't seen your artwork, so you are the only judge of its merit." Catherine lifted her shoulders. "If you don't have faith in it . . ." her voice faded with meaning.

"It's not that!" Tiana defended herself. "It's just . . . well, it seems so unorthodox to put them in without an okay."

"You should realize by now things rarely get done routinely. Look at the way you stumbled into the Avery contract. Look at the way Peter works! That should tell you something about this business," argued Catherine.

"I suppose you're right," Tiana conceded. But still she felt a tinge of foreboding. Why was she hesitating? Catherine knew how things were done. She wouldn't lead her astray. Would she? No! Tiana dismissed the thought immediately. Catherine was simply too nice and besides she would be a partner in the event. That decided it. "All right, I'll do it!"

"You won't regret it! Do you want to go over now?" Catherine asked.

"Might as well, before I change my mind."

"You won't have any trouble getting into the office. One of the security people will let you in. Just get the doorman to flag you a cab," Catherine instructed.

"Aren't you coming?" Tiana asked with a rising note of disquiet.

"I would but I just remembered a call I'm waiting for and I'd hate to miss it. You'll be okay. There's nothing to it," Catherine soothed.

A short time later Tiana discovered Catherine had been right about getting into the building. There was a guard on duty in the lobby. He checked her identification against an employee roster and waved her through after she signed the log. Tiana then used her own key to get into Peter's office where she picked up her sketches but found no file of the other ideas.

After locking Peter's office, Tiana paused to consider her next move. Her indecision was resolved by the shuffling approach of a cleaning woman as she pulled the carriage of an industrial pail behind her rotund form.

With an unholy commitment, Tiana asked, "Excuse me, could you open the door to Mr. Dahlquist's office? I want to see if a file is in there."

The woman eyed Tiana rather like a goldfish looking out from its glass prison. Tiana thought the woman was going to refuse but then she made a grudging movement of her head which Tiana took for agreement.

The woman heaved a pained sigh and then trundled back down the hall. She took no more than ten steps when she turned and spoke her first words to Tiana. "Are you coming?"

"Yes! Oh yes!" Tiana scampered to close the distance between them. When they reached the door to Bayne's outer office, Tiana waited with growing impatience for the cleaning woman to open the door. The same tense procedure was repeated when she unlocked his private office. As the door swung open, she thanked the woman for her help, only to see her already moving away.

Left alone in Bayne's private office, Tiana had probably never felt less sure of herself. A glance at the cleared top of his executive desk told her the missing file was not there. A survey of the room revealed there were no files laying casually about anywhere. If it was here at all there was only one possible place it could be. Inside Bayne's desk! Unnecessarily tip-toeing across the room, Tiana went behind the large desk. Quietly laying her folder on the inlaid surface of it, she gave the top drawer a gentle tug. When it did not open, she exerted a little more force. The result was the same. It remained closed. She repeated the procedure for each drawer but they were all locked against her entry.

Without realizing it, Tiana had been holding her breath. Once she discovered the desk was locked, the air left her lungs in an explosion of relief paired with groundless frustration. Straightening her back, she picked up her folder from the top of the desk. Perhaps she could look in the secretary's office. Suddenly an ungodly shiver danced over her skin, chilling her to the marrow. Turning her head sideways Tiana knew instinctively it was not the cleaning lady she would see. An audible cry was torn from her parted lips as her eyes found Bayne.

He was leaning against the side of the entrance. His arms were carelessly crossed in front of him as a shoulder was pressed against the doorjamb. How long he had been there watching her would forever be his secret.

He ignited a feeling in Tiana which flamed into unprecedented fear as she sought unsuccessfully to stop the trembling of her limbs, but her nerveless fingers refused to obey. She dropped the folder! It bounced on the soft carpeting, spilling its contents grotesquely in a condemnation of her guilt.

Appalled, she knelt to retrieve the drawings, scrabbling to reclaim the evidence of her duplicity.

All to no avail! The highly polished tips of Bayne's leather shoes intruded into her peripheral vision. Bowing her head lower, Tiana prayed the floor would open up and swallow her whole, but it did not. That would have been too merciful! She took far longer than was absolutely necessary to gather the papers together. Stacking and aligning them with a compulsive precision, Tiana played out the filament of time for all it was worth.

Finally, when she could do nothing else, Tiana rose quiveringly to her feet. Her guilt-ridden eyes remained downcast, shyly hiding from the silent reproach she was sure to find in his. "I know how this must look. But it isn't what you think."

"And exactly what is it I'm supposed to think?" Oddly there was no stigmatizing censure in his voice, only mild curiosity; mysteriously absent was any trace of anger.

Her head came up. She met his gaze unflinchingly although a fierce battle was still being waged in her stomach. "I know it must look like I'm some kind of thief, but I'm not! I only came in here to see if the Asgard file was in your office. I did some drawings that I thought might be added to the others, but I couldn't find them in Peter's office and so I thought they might be in here. It was the only other place I could think to look."

"After hours?" One brow crooked with serene interest.

It was enough to send her flimsy pretense of confidence spattering in all directions! No longer able to meet the steadiness in his gaze, Tiana glanced down at the folder. "I'm sorry I missed the deadline. I meant to show them to Peter but forgot until a short while ago. We tried to call him but there was no answer. I guess I should have waited until Monday." Her voice dissolved in the constriction of her throat as misery flooded through her.

"As a matter of fact Monday would have been too late. We sent our package over at closing today."

"Oh!" Nervously, Tiana began to roll the edges of the folder. She was justly punished and her eyes remained fixed on the curling papers. "I see. Then I was too late."

"A realist would have to say so!"

Her head shot up at the untimely amusement in his voice. The corner of his mouth twitched in a spell of undisguised enjoyment, as he said, "I returned Catherine's call apparently right after you left, missing you by minutes. So I swung by here to intercept you."

Tiana's hampered breathing eased as she sighed in heartfelt relief. "You knew all the time?"

"Yes! I wanted to see how you intended to extricate yourself. You looked so guilty and flustered that I couldn't resist."

Despite being let off the hook, or maybe because of the way in which Bayne did it, Tiana's foot scuffed at the lush pile of the carpet. "You didn't have to come at me like some menacing devil!" Annoyance crowded the heels of her retreating guilt.

Laughing, Bayne said, "Did I really look like a devil to you?"

"Yes!" Her gaze slid away from the merriment shining in his.

"Only because you felt so guilty." He pointed out with insular jauntiness.

Bayne Dahlquist had the distinctive and altogether intolerable knack for crumbling her resolve! Without meaning it to, her distracted vision floated back to him. "*Only* because you always jump to the wrong conclusions about me."

"Do I?" Amusement winked out from his words as his lips smoothed to an unbending line. His green eyes glimmered with a light flirtation.

All cognitive thought deserted her as he awaited her response with annoying patience. "Yes," she mumbled self-consciously.

"What do you intend to do about it?" His eyes traveled gravely over the tensed features of her face.

"I . . . nothing. What could I do to change your impressions? You've already made up your mind about me." Her voice was low but carried in the stillness of the office.

A tight smile pulled at the corners of his mouth. "Have I? I'm not so sure anymore," he said more to himself than to her.

If Bayne's ulterior motive was to confuse her, to lead her down the convoluted path of perplexity, he succeeded past the bounds of decency. She knew what he thought of her and her idealism! He had certainly told her often enough! But something in the hazy implication of his admission vibrated within her like a tuning fork, sending ever larger shockwaves through her.

Bisected as she was by conflicting information, Tiana pushed it behind the curtain of conscious thought. She would deal with it later without all the pressure of Bayne's presence. "I guess I had better be going." Once committed to the words, she stepped away from him and moved toward . . . the door.

"What about your artwork?"

Her walk slowed but did not stop. "You said the others had already been sent over."

"Right! But I never said it was too late to send over yours as well."

The unvoiced promise halted her. She turned to him almost afraid to trust in her hope. Then because he refused to pave her way, she asked, "Would you?"

"Would I what?" He came around the desk. As he leaned back against the front of it, his hands were buttressed at his sides.

His deliberate pretense of not understanding her caused Tiana to change bearing. "You wouldn't send mine over?"

"Why not?" A deceptive laziness invaded his manner. He was toying with her, extending an invitation for her to continue with their verbal sparring.

"You don't even know if they're any good," she countered, coolly attempting to fight the warmth suffusing her body, a growing heat he was responsible for creating.

The grooves next to his mouth deepened in devilry. "Suppose you tell me. Are they any good?"

"I think so!" She met his gaze bravely, not faltering at the reproving mirth.

"Then I believe you."

She rapidly blinked back her surprise. "You mean you think they are good?"

"No, I believe you think they are good." His tone was pillowed with light sarcasm.

Disappointment and, yes, sadness shadowed her eyes. When would she learn not to take the bait of his mockery? She could not defeat his cynicism. It was too much a part of him! "If you don't think they are any good, why even consider sending them?"

"I could justify it for many reasons. We often send

over straw men, deliberate diversions, ideas that are not serious contenders for a contract. The reasons vary. It could be so the client has something to reject, or to show them how many people are working on the account, or even to demonstrate our earnestness although we may not have come up with anything viable. Sometimes these ideas buy us time, sometimes they don't." He shrugged, making no attempt to soften his explanation.

Unable to conceal her bruised reaction, Tiana bent her head. "Then I would prefer you not send mine over." She employed every ounce of her willpower in not allowing her voice to crack but she was not able to keep the betraying weakness from its volume.

"I've hurt your feelings, haven't I?" he said in a rough whisper. "It is true what I told you about straw men designs; sometimes—for some clients. I wanted to show you that no matter how well we plan and execute a concept, there is no accounting for the way some firms decide on a promotional idea. There are as many different ways of settling on an advertising campaign as there are client companies and advertising agencies." He drew a long breath. "So you see, what I personally like often has little bearing on the eventual decision of the client. I inferred your drawings would be sent over as straw men simply because Peter hasn't seen them and because we already formed our package. But if it will make you feel any better, I do like your sketches."

Cautiously, she raised her head. "But you haven't even seen them."

"I had ample opportunity to see them while you were picking them up from the floor," he reminded her.

Curiosity ate voraciously at her pride, so much so, that she could not prevent herself from asking, "Did you really like them?"

"They are as good as anything else we have sent

them. Here, give me the folder before you tear them to pieces." He extended a hand, effectively bankrupting her indecision.

Quickly she smoothed the curled cover before giving him the drawings. Even the teeth catching at her lower lip could not inhibit her pleased smile. "Thank you! I don't know what else to say except thank you."

Steadfastly, Bayne's eyes torched over her as he placed the folder on the desk. "There is nothing else to say." His voice was a courier for some as yet unspoken thought. He reached to lift Tiana's hand from where it lay at her side. "It's a pity."

Her eyes clung to his. "What is?"

"Your hair!" he sighed. "I never even got to put my fingers through that long bewitching glory before it was cut off. A pity."

For one cataclysmic instant her heart stopped beating! He noticed her appearance! He was not unmoved by the change! Then when her heart began its rhythm again it was with a joyful leap, the blood cavorting through her veins.

The fraudulently casual stance of his body embedded a double-edged sword within her. One part wanted to merge closer to surrender to his seduction. The other half shyly stood in awe of the supreme masculine enticement.

"Tiana," the enthralling gauntlet of his voice tempted her even as the glittering rogue in his eyes should have cautioned her. With a masterful stroke of decisiveness, Bayne pulled her to him.

So bid, Tiana's gaze was inexorably drawn to the compelling line of his sentient mouth. As his arms encircled her yielding body, her lips followed the trail blazed by her eyes as she unquestionably obeyed his silent command.

Provisional contact, as her mouth met his, was so faint, so light as to be reminiscent of a sultry summer day, unrushed in its timelessness. Sure and yet unsure, Tiana experimented with the heady implosion of feeling. And he allowed it, until those first flutterings of her uncertainty were replaced with something more meaningful and alive. His mouth conveyed a new order as his lips parted hers with unrivaled expertise. As her mouth opened to his, Tiana succumbed with an eager willingness. She was possessed by a craving so strong, so demanding as to be rendered almost mindless in his promissory embrace.

Her hands found their anchor at the tapering muscles of his waist. All rational thought was banished as she offered her will at the temple of desire by returning his kiss.

The tactician in him let his hand play along the sensitized column of her spine, molding her consenting flesh to his need and turning her bones liquid. Under the exploratory search of her fingers as they traveled the distance of his back, his body hardened; the taut, sinewy muscles barely leashing the primitive strength within. Every cell in her body burned as the bonds of control were loosened.

With an urgent restlessness, his hands investigated her slender back and then following the flowing lines of her hips downward shaped her assenting body to his length.

Brought against the bold contours of his male body, the last lingering kernel of restraint melted and her flesh fused with his. Like softened wax her body was imprinted with the passion of his demand. When his lips left hers to forge a pathway across her cheek to her ear, a shuddering moan escaped as a new wave of pleasure washed over her. His mouth claimed new

territory as he nibbled the delicate lobe of her ear
sending blind quivers of delight through her as she was
carried to yet another plane of sensation. With an
embarrassing lack of inhibition, Tiana witnessed the
last of her control slip away as his hand came up to
circle her breast.

Nothing in her possession could have halted her
runaway emotions when, out of the stillness, the air was
rent with a grievous mechanical growl as a machine
came to life in the outer office. With a cry of alarm,
Tiana sprang to free herself from the suffocating ring of
his arms. A strangled sound was in her throat as Tiana
glanced over her shoulder toward the other room
where she feared she would see the cleaning woman.
Although Tiana did not see the woman, her presence
was confirmed by the steady whine of a vacuum.

Tiana stiffened at the mental picture of her momentary abandonment, at the way she had surrendered to
Bayne's will without so much as a second's hesitation.

A distant smile played on Bayne's mouth, dallied
there a little and then faded as his arms opened to
release her.

The impatient sound of the cleaning woman in the
outer office served as an uncalled-for reminder to Tiana
of her excessively awkward position. Her eyes darted
nervously around the room, fearful of making contact
with his, lest she fall victim to his devastating appeal
again. Accordingly, her hands twisted together in front
of her.

"I hope you aren't waiting for an apology," Bayne
asked in a low pitched voice that could not suppress the
irony of the question.

No! Never an apology! Tiana knew from painful
experience, he would never apologize. Besides, in this
situation, it would be a travesty against nature, against

the woman Tiana had been in his arms. Why should he apologize for his behavior any more than she should apologize for her response?

"Because it is not my fault that we were interrupted." Then Bayne continued with more than a silk screen of humor, "I can promise you there will be no interruptions if you come to Connecticut with me for the weekend."

Like a thousand bee stings his callous offer knocked her senseless. It had only been a physical exercise with him. He had shown such desire, such passion and even those first few moments of unreserved tenderness, Tiana had thought—no, that was just it, she had not thought. The moment was past and best be forgotten. It had all been a carefully executed illusion! And she had been fooled into thinking he cared. But it would not happen again! Never again! Her voice was wraithlike, a disembodied spirit of its former self. "I couldn't. I moved in with Catherine only an hour ago and haven't even unpacked."

"Leave it." He studied her for a frozen instant and then exhaled wearily. "Never mind. Forget what I said. Come on, I'll give you a lift home."

Mutely, she nodded her agreement and he turned to retrieve the folder. On the short ride over to Fifth Avenue the silence stretched between them like the limitless grasslands of the American prairie; undulating and rippling with a teeming life of its own while maintaining its singular entity. They were two individual and separate people and yet there was between them that which was uniquely whole.

Tiana could not speak for Bayne. But as for herself, she knew something strange and wonderful had happened. She could not forget the cruelty of his mockery or the vastness of their differences. But there was something greater than those things. The heavenly deity knew she had never meant it to happen, had never wanted it to happen, but it had and there was nothing she could do about it. She loved him! She loved Bayne! Beyond all bounds and limits into the distant recesses of her dreams, she loved him!

Chapter Seven

Not once but twice, Tiana had managed to wiggle out
of accepting Bayne's too-tempting invitation to spend a
weekend with him. Now as she stood alone in the
kitchen of Bayne's restored farmhouse in Redding,
Connecticut, Tiana pondered the turn of events and the
twisting circumstances that led her here.

It was scarcely more than a week since her last
refusal, a week filled with grueling hours modeling
before the camera. And model she did! In every
conceivable way, with every imaginable prop. Tiana had
posed and posed and posed! She had been photographed in, on, around, and under giant mushrooms,
trees, meadows, and misty machine-made clouds. Her
form-fitting costume had become a second skin. It
consisted of a basic one piece body stocking in luminescent pearl green. Sometimes over it, she donned a
wispy skirt of transparent material of an irregular
length, somewhat suggestive of leaves.

Although Tiana had unfailingly done her best during
the long sessions in the studio, it apparently had not
been enough. The day before, Peter had come to her,
telling her that they had not been able to get the picture
they were looking for and so wanted to experiment with
some location shots. Readily, she agreed and then

could have bitten her tongue out when Peter explained he intended to use Bayne's property in Connecticut. When Tiana resisted, Peter attempted to reassure her by saying they would not be alone. Catherine and Bayne would also be there. And when she persistently tried to squirm out of going, Peter simply reminded her that she was under contract and had no choice but to go.

Admittedly it had not been as bad as Tiana had feared. On the way north, the foursome had traveled together and Bayne had made no reference to the fact that she was en route to his house. It was then Tiana decided to relax and enjoy the outing. The lush green hills of the country were a pleasant change from the city.

When Peter entered the kitchen with his typical casual alertness, he announced, "I'm going out to scout possible locations with Catherine. Do you want to come along?"

"Not unless you need me," Tiana answered.

After Peter and Catherine left, Tiana went to her assigned room to change the rose-colored pantsuit she had worn on the trip. She replaced it with her favorite pair of denim jeans and a long-sleeved plaid shirt, whose ends were allowed to hang over her slim hips. Bayne was busy in his den with paperwork and Tiana yielded to the irresistible urge to explore outside. The afternoon, a balmy one free of pollution, beckoned with the mystique of all such days.

Aimlessly, she walked around the yard until she accidentally stumbled on a marked trail rubbed into the hillside near the house. Without conscious thought, Tiana took it. She had not traveled far when she heard her name called. Tiana stopped but deliberately did not turn around. She recognized Bayne's voice and for some reason, she was not surprised he had abandoned his work. No one could resist such a day! Her ears strained to hear the sound of his approaching footfalls.

"I thought you might like some company and a guide, since you don't know your way around. Do you mind if I join you?" Bayne inquired in his own rhetorical way.

"Please." Her throat closed over the word prohibiting any other comment as she turned to face him. Forgotten was her need to be alone as her eyes took in his ruggedly masculine appearance. One hand was thrust carelessly into the pocket of his corded pants, emphasizing his dominant male potency while serving to maintain a distinctively casual stance. He wore a pale gold pullover shirt that did not conceal the rippling muscles beneath in any discernible way.

As he walked abreast of her, Tiana wondered if she would be able to keep the caprice from her senses and the vagrant song from her heart. The path, slowly, gracefully unfurled in front of them steadily upwards. But the feeling that unwound within Tiana was not anywhere as distinct as the ground before them. For she carried with her the memories of other times, other places, when Bayne had been with her. And those memories dodged around her willpower with the resiliency of fire against air. Maddeningly, the more she tried to exert control, the higher the blaze!

Tiana's eyes doggedly ran along the course of the beaten earth. When the woods thickened, they could no longer travel side by side. Bayne forged ahead, his extended arms and taller frame keeping the branches and leaves from striking Tiana. They walked in silence as if by mutual agreement. Before long the trail disappeared and Tiana found they were enclosed on all sides by the invading vegetation; beech and ash trees formed the walls of their world. Her footing, at the best precarious, hesitated as she became aware of the subtle intimacy of the environment.

At her faltering stride, Bayne half turned and waited for her to catch up. "It isn't much further." His eyes, green and sparkling, journeyed the distance to settle on her face.

She erased the space between them and apologized. "I'm sorry, I didn't mean to lag behind." Her own gaze was held by his.

"There's no hurry." He smiled down at her before resuming the lead.

Tiana fell in with his unhurried pace, noticing he had slowed his steps. Ravenously her eyes took in his vibrant form; the wide span of shoulders tapering to a lean waist, the long muscular legs and the occasional abridged glimpse of his distinctive profile. Tiana sighed deeply, not so much from the sylvan appeal of her surroundings as from the unaccountable feeling welling within her.

At the slight sound she must have made, Bayne checked his stride and pivoted toward her in one linear motion. "Tiana?"

Her name, an unanswered question, hung in the air. Her brown eyes fastened on the long remembered features of his lean face. But the abrupt raucous calling of a bird overhead caused her eyes to veer away searching the foliage for the source. Purposefully she scanned the overhanging branches in a futile attempt to locate the animal whose strident cry had pierced the stillness.

Bayne lifted an arm, his index finger pointed up towards the right. Tiana followed the direction but failed to sight the bird. His other hand came up behind her to position her head, moving closer so that she could focus along the length of his upraised arm. She saw the bird! It was a blue jay, bobbing excitedly. An instant later, it took refuge into denser leafage.

A smile of unanticipated pleasure touched her mouth. She lifted her eyes to thank Bayne as his hand slipped unconsciously to her shoulder. Although a ghost of a smile lingered on his mouth, the eyes that studied her were thoughtful.

An impatient breeze tumbled her hair into a ruffled cap and teased the color into her translucent skin as her eyes locked with his. A wordless poem, as old as the ages, passed between them. And her smile fled at the driving onslaught of desire sweeping through her. Fluid flames licked her veins in meter to the erotic imagery of love's poem.

So powerful was the message, Tiana began to quiver at its significance. Bayne brought his other hand to her shoulder, turning her fully to the solid length of his body. While both hands bracketed her shoulders, his thumbs drifted tantalizingly over the delicate column of her throat. Her pulse danced like wildfire! Her senses clamored! His gaze speared her, prolonging the inevitable moment to painful intensity. Until finally, his mouth descended.

They moved together in unified motion pressing bodies fevered with longing into a closer embrace. Her hands came up to imprison the broad expanse of his back, reveling in the feel of the taut muscles straining beneath the confines of his shirt. Bayne wrapped his arms around her. It was a sublime explosion of complete communication; a sharing which transcended the physical and soared into the nether world of the spirit.

As they paid homage to the god of desire, time spun away in meaningless disarray. She scarcely felt him lift her in his arms as he lowered her to the bracken-covered earth. Leaves fallen in past seasons took his weight as his body joined hers. One muscular leg tangled between hers as his hands cupped her face to sprinkle kisses across her nose, cheeks, and cyelids.

"Bayne!" The name was a crying moan from within.

He answered her plea without words. His warm mouth crept to the hollow of her neck as he edged back the collar of her shirt. But that only satisfied him temporarily. Soon, he levered himself up, one hand wedged between them as his practiced fingers unbuttoned her shirt with consummate ease. His voice roughened as his lips moved downward to the rounded curve of her breast. "I've wanted you like this since the first moment I saw you!" he groaned. "How I want you!"

Panic-stricken, Tiana's head moved restlessly in unfamiliar turmoil. It was as much from raw desire as from the cinemagraphic picture playing on the screen of her mind. So, he had wanted her in yielding abandon since the first time he saw her! How like Bayne! It confirmed her worst fears! Yes, he wanted her but only as a momentary diversion based on nothing more than physical need. Nothing had changed! There had never been any words of love between them! And there never would be!

Suddenly Tiana became aware of the dampened earth beneath her. Her spine stiffened. The realization that it had made no difference only a short time ago hit her like a blow between the eyes. In one convulsive movement, Tiana twisted away from Bayne. Scrambling to her feet, she pulled her plaid shirt back over her shoulders.

She kept her back resolutely squared to him. The quavering of her limbs would not cease as she gulped down great drafts of air. Buttons became monstrous things, refusing to obediently fit into tiny holes as her shaking fingers forced them to comply. Untamed emotion erupted in huge sobbing waves within her. She swallowed down the urge to cry. Tiana would not weep in front of the man who had unknowingly caused it all! The pain, the desire, the happiness, and the sorrow were all part of her love for Bayne!

When all the fastenings were closed, she dropped her hands to her side. She sensed Bayne move to stand behind her. She had to bite her lower lip to remove the sensual pleasure.

Bayne made no motion to touch her. His voice caressed, "What happened Tiana? Did I go too fast for you?"

"No, no, I . . . I changed my mind," she stuttered, barely able to keep her voice from cracking and shattering under the writhing tension.

"Obviously!" The unconstrained sarcasm was again a recognizable part of him. "What I want to know is why."

Under the indictment of his persistence, her head bowed low. Her chin nearly brushing her chest.

"Tiana? Why?" His unfailing perseverance echoed in the weight of the inquiry.

"I changed my mind," she whispered brokenly. The excuse was not worthy of repetition but she could think of nothing else to say. What could she say to satisfy his determination to know? Not the truth! He would never understand or forgive her the truth. He would put her love down as yet another example of her hopeless romanticism.

He heaved an exasperated sigh. "So you've already said. Now to repeat myself, why?"

Her head remained down as she closed her eyes against the scalding tears. Her passionate desire had been transformed to a cache of damaged pride, physical frustration, and steadfast yearning. For in spite of everything, her body still called out for his.

"Tiana?" This time her name was murmured near her ear.

Sensing danger, her head jerked up. "I changed my mind," she repeated tonelessly.

"There has to be a reason." Pragmatism scored the edges of his question. "You wanted it as much as I did."

"I can't deny it!" Color crept into her tone. "Yes, I wanted you but not anymore, not now. My body wanted yours but not my mind."

With an irritated curse, he spun her around to face his fury. Something dangerous glinted in his eyes. "You fool! Since when do a man and woman make love with their minds? Even you, in your ivory tower, can't be that naive." He clearly expected no reply as disgust contorted his features. "There is no rhythm or reason for the feeling between a man and a woman. Why fight nature?"

Unseeing, Tiana was long past the threshold of pain. Her eyes, glassy with unshed tears, stared ahead without blinking. "I have no intention of discussing it with you." Her voice was as cold and as lifeless as her eyes.

"For once we agree! Right now talk is the last thing I want from you," Bayne crushed her to his body, infusing her with the venom of his words in a brutal, punishing kiss. There was no mistaking his desperate hunger. She could not fight him, not with words and not with her body. She went limp in his arms refusing to give honor to his insult.

Bayne released her then, but not completely. One hand curled around the back of her neck, strong fingers laced through her hair. He hauled her head back glaring into fear-widened eyes. And in the next instant she was free and he was no longer touching her. "Tiana? Tiana, won't you tell me what's the matter?"

The tenderness, the pleading note so uncharacteristic of him proved to be her complete undoing. The tears in her eyes flashed like twin jewels. "Did it ever occur to you that I don't like rutting around in the woods like some animal. I expect more than that."

"So, that's it! Quite frankly, no, it never crossed my mind. But then why should you be any different from other women?" His eyes glittered ominously. "What will it be then? Moonlight and roses? A yacht anchored off the coast? A suite at the Plaza? Name it and you've got it!"

Frozen contemptuously in his glare, Tiana could do nothing more than gasp at the sickening interpretation he had put on her words. She wanted more than a desperate coupling with him. She wanted the impossibility of his love. But he could never understand. He had immediately put a sordid price tag on her statement, making it seem as if she wanted only the trappings of romance. They were less than a foot apart and yet they stood at opposite ends of the universe.

He squinted at her, his eyes a brittle flame. "Shy? Reticent? Come, come, surely you have some idea of what it is you want! Or am I to guess?" he sneered wickedly.

"No," she mumbled. "No." The word came quietly against the hurt building inside of her.

"You don't want me guessing. Then tell me, what is it you want from me?" The quiet menace in his voice struck a shaft of terror in her heart.

"Stop it! Stop it!" Her hands covered her ears.

Steel fingers gripped her wrists, ripping her hands from her ears. "Why, so you can crawl back into your dreamworld? Tell me what you want! Tell me what it takes to reach you!"

"Don't you mean *buy* me?" Her voice flattened to a shadow of its former self.

"What do you mean?" he asked. "How can I buy you when I don't even know how to reach you?"

Tiana tried to no avail to pull her hands from his relentless hold. "Let me alone! I don't want you near me. I don't want anything to do with you!" she lied.

"Why not?" he demanded tightening his fingers until Tiana thought her bones would snap.

"I have everything I want! I don't need you to get what I want!" Her voice caught on a silent sob.

"What is it you want? I don't think you know!" he jeered with refined viciousness. "Once you told me you wanted to be a commercial artist. Now you have given all that up to be a model. What is it you want?"

She could not tell him that she had agreed to model, in part, for him, to help his advertising agency retain an important contract. He wouldn't believe her anyway. "I still want to be an artist."

"That's why you signed a modeling contract," he said with lethal sarcasm. "I told you once that to pursue a goal as an artist was demanding and you weren't capable of making the sacrifices. Do you seriously think the sacrifices in becoming a model are any less crippling? You profess to know your own mind and yet you change goals with the thoughtless ease of the very young. Since you obviously don't know what it is you really want or need, why not let me help you! I can do a lot for you."

"Oh—Oh! How can you be so cruel?" Her eyes were a liquid brown as the tears gathered again.

"Is it cruel to speak the truth?" Then he relented, his voice softening, "Tiana?"

Furiously, Tiana blinked back the tears. With all her slight weight she pulled against the manacles of his fingers. "You're hurting me. Please let me go."

Surprised, Bayne glanced down at her wrists. Immediately his fingers sprung open to free her. "I didn't realize . . ." He sounded oddly repentant.

But Tiana had no time to mull over the significance of his gentled voice. With all speed she snatched back her hands, rubbing at the sore wrists. Her head bent down as if the task took all of her attention. "I want to get out of here. Just tell me which way to go." And then as an apparent afterthought, "Please!" she begged without really meaning to at all.

"I'll take you out," he said resignedly. "Will you follow me?"

She nodded her head and waited for him to take the first step before falling in behind him. His back was turned to her and she used the chance to wipe a stray tear from the corner of her eye. She sniffled and was grateful when no other tears followed. They walked in tandem until they were out of the woods and had reached the edge of a meadow which ran up the side of the hill. The clearing was lined on both sides by a wide stone fence three feet high.

Bayne stepped lithely to the top of the large grey fieldstones forming the low border. He turned, offering a helping hand to Tiana. She did not hesitate before trusting her hand to his. With his other hand placed under her elbow, Bayne pulled her atop the fence before springing to the other side with innate grace.

When she thought he might extend his supporting hand again, Tiana was surprised to feel him brace a lifting hold on her waist. His hands spanned her waist without difficulty. They were no longer in the dappled shade of the trees and Tiana could clearly see his expression as she gazed down into his upturned face. He paused, his eyes freely scrutinizing her. The recent discord fell away as he silently worked his spell on her. Her heart lurched as he lifted her only to keep her suspended in the air. Contrary to all the laws of biology and in spite of the bright sunlight, her eyes dilated as they were lost in his.

"Tiana." It was a wish on his lips as he slowly, deliberately lowered her. Her hands rested lightly on his shoulders as he drew her inexorably towards him. Scant inches separated them! And even those were too much!

"Ho there! Bayne! Tiana! Wait up you two!" Peter's hail and hearty greeting split the atmosphere with a crackling force. His interruption ruptured the scene with the subtleness of gunfire and with about the same reception.

Half slithering, half falling, Tiana groaned inwardly as she hit the earth with a jarring thud. Unaccustomed shock waves of pain coursed through her ankle. She automatically reached down to sooth the injured area. As she did so, Tiana caught a glimpse of Peter plodding up the hill, Catherine in his wake. Absentmindedly, Tiana continued to finger her ankle.

"Did you hurt yourself?" Bayne asked solicitously.

Looking up through the dark fringe of her lashes, Tiana replied, "No, it's just a little wrench. It's all right, really!" And to prove it, she stood erect, testing it with her weight. With only a slight twinge, it held fine, the smarting discomfort all but gone.

He spared her a mocking glance. "There was no need to jump out of my arms or did you think Peter would have something to say about it?"

Without taking her eyes from the pair climbing the hill, she said tartly, "No!" Tiana licked her parched lips, realizing they were swollen. Whether from Bayne's ardent kisses or her own punitive biting, she could not decide. The other couple was rapidly removing the distance separating them. Quickly Tiana smoothed the clinging folds of her rumpled shirt before running clammy hands over the legs of her jeans.

"Catherine! Hammett!" Bayne nodded to each. "Did you find anything interesting?"

"Ah, yes!" Catherine purred happily as she adjusted the leather strap of her camera. "We found a glorious ravine! Peter thinks he can use it as a location for some of the shots of Tiana. We also discovered a marvelous patch of wood violets. But Peter is afraid they wouldn't show up very well in an ad. Have you found anything?"

Not quite meeting Catherine's eyes, Tiana felt a slight flush steal up her cheeks. After what seemed an interminable length of time Bayne answered, "We weren't actually looking. However, we were on our way to Look-Out-Point. You might want to consider it."

"It sounds intriguing! Where is it?" Catherine used her forefinger to slide a pair of sunglasses back to the bridge of her nose.

Stretching out an arm, Bayne pointed in an upland direction. "There it is, near the top of the hill."

Three pairs of interested eyes swiveled to the hilltop where they could see the implacable outline of jutting grey boulders against the final rise. Nature had surely created a remarkable fortification with the sculptured massing of giant rocks. Sometime in the distant past, when ponderous glaciers had crawled over this section of the earth, numerous such outcroppings had been originated. Today they existed as a remarkable testimony of a bygone age.

"Hmmm." Peter's gaze narrowed. "Let's go up and have a look!"

A flirting breeze cooled the warm sunshine so the climb was accomplished in relative, if not total comfort. Tiana was more than a little grateful for the presence of the other couple. She shuddered to think of what might have happened had they not arrived when they did. Would she always respond so uncontrollably to Bayne? No, she pushed the thought from her mind. For her own sake and for Catherine's, she must not allow herself to be alone with Bayne in the future.

For Tiana the exalted view of the valley from the cluster of boulders was anticlimactical after the panorama of emotion she had been exposed to that afternoon. She said all the appreciative adjectives and made all the appropriate sounds of pleasure along with the others but somehow hers lacked any erstwhile conviction. After the viewing from Look-Out-Point, they all decided to return to the house.

Once inside, Tiana did not stop to join the others for refreshments but pleaded an uncontested headache and fled to her room. She had been buffeted and tumbled from the latest skirmish with Bayne and had not completely recovered. She had to lodge distance and time between herself and Bayne. And in truth, her temples did throb with every rhythmical beat of her heart.

Tiana sank down on her bed with the express purpose of thinking over everything that had happened in the last few hours. She needed to think, to plan! There was so much to sort through. She had the most admirable of intentions so it was with a keen sense of irritation that she opened her eyes to discover she had fallen asleep. The lengthening shadows in the room told her that she had indeed been napping.

After slipping on her shoes and combing her hair, Tiana emerged to find Peter alone in the living room. He was slouched over the coffee table with a calculated array of photographic equipment spread before him. His elbows were supported on his parted knees as his fingers diligently worked a scrap of material around a lens. He glanced up at her entrance. "Well, if it isn't our resident sleepyhead, come to join the land of the living!"

She grimaced, dismissing his kidding without a sound as she eased into one of the armchairs.

"I peeked into your room," Peter confessed sheepishly, "and saw you were dead to the world. How's the headache?"

"Gone! But I didn't mean to fall asleep. I guess I was tired and didn't realize it."

Peter replaced the lens and picked up another one from the table. Again, with a circular motion, he began to wipe. "You have been under a lot of stress lately. You know what they say, it never rains but it pours!"

Tiana smiled, entering the easy mood of bantering. "If that's not the truth, then I don't know what is."

"Speaking as your photographer, I'm glad you caught a few winks. This afternoon, you looked like you had just about had it."

"This afternoon? What do you mean?" Suddenly alert, Tiana sat up, her neck held stiffly.

Quizzically fixing his eyes on her, Peter said with a delusive casualness, "Oh, I don't know. I thought perhaps you and Bayne had some kind of falling out."

"Falling out?" Taken aback by his statement, Tiana could not help but become an echo. How did he know? He could just be fishing! Tiana made a belated effort to gather her wits. "Why would you say such a thing?"

Peter lifted his shoulders. "I thought you looked disturbed." He glanced at her sideways. "Hey, you weren't mad because we joined you, were you?"

"No! Of course not!" Tiana felt the color creeping into her face.

"So, if you weren't angry with us, that leaves only Bayne." His attention had gone back to his equipment but then his head bobbed up as he finished. "And I know from experience any disagreement you might have had with Bayne would not have been over business. Which means it had to be something personal. Add to that other factors and I would swear it was . . . ah . . . romantic."

She gasped aloud as her eyes widened. She had not expected this. Peter had gone for the jugular! Then with a concentrated effort to regain her composure, she attempted a bluff, "No-no! You're wrong. There was no disagreement, either business or personal."

"No romantic interlude either, I suppose," Peter observed with salty sarcasm. He leaned back in his seat, the ankle of one long leg positioned atop the other knee while he observed her.

As if Peter were holding a magnifying glass to her, Tiana felt she was a moth pinned down for examination. She felt naked and vulnerable as fragile emotions were held up for inspection. Her eyes, cloudy with confusion, skipped disjointedly around the room, taking in the bookcase that fronted one entire wall, the massive fireplace and finally dropping forlornly to the wooden floor.

"You're really troubled, aren't you?" Peter asked in surprise.

Debating whether to try for a denial, Tiana settled on a portion of the truth. "Yes, only because I don't know what to say to you."

"You don't owe me any explanation. You want to roll around in the hay with Bayne, that's your business," he said expressionlessly.

"But I didn't!" she cried in shock. "We didn't! How could you even suggest such a thing?"

"I'm a photographer and by nature I'm observant. If I didn't see things that other people missed I wouldn't be very successful," he explained calmly. "You and Bayne walk out of the woods, he looks at you questioningly and you avoid his eyes at every opportunity. Both of you are suspiciously quiet and withdrawn. And . . ." he paused . . . "I didn't really think you got those leaves and twigs in your hair from laying on the ground all by yourself."

She swallowed, digesting Peter's stark revelation. Her eyes inched back to him, a question nesting there. If Peter knew, who else did?

"What is it?" Peter read the fear in her hunted eyes.

"Will you say anything?" Terror was her whispering voice.

"To whom? Bayne? Catherine?"

She nodded nervously.

Peter leaned forward. "Why would I say anything? What's to say?"

She caught her lower lip between her teeth. "I don't know."

With a face set in crafty thought, Peter's eyes roamed freely over her. Lines of unrestrained speculation grooved his forehead. "Don't worry, Tiana, I know when to keep quiet."

Tiana exhaled in relief. She knew it was not a part of Peter's nature to delve deeply into the motives of others. Tiana knew she could trust his silence. As far as she was concerned the subject was closed. "Where are the others?"

"Uh, what?" Peter said abstractly. Although his gaze was still on Tiana, it was plain his thoughts were elsewhere. So she repeated the question.

"Oh! In the kitchen getting dinner," he answered and only nodded when Tiana said she would go and see if they wanted any help.

As she pushed open the door to the kitchen, Tiana

had second thoughts. She could hear the murmur of their voices and as the door moved, the conversation stopped. Since she had evidently been noticed she had no choice but to enter all the way.

"You're up!" Catherine smiled. "Bayne and I were just discussing whether or not we should wake you for dinner. How are you feeling?"

"Fine!" Tiana responded with more animation than she felt. She was fanatically aware of Bayne's tall figure as he stood next to Catherine. He was so lean and powerful, his mere presence seemed to shrink the room. She wanted to fix her gaze on him, to devour him with her eyes. But instead she looked at Catherine and inquired brightly, "Can I do anything to help?"

"Not a thing!" Catherine's eyes slid to Bayne. "We have everything under control. We're having spaghetti. Hope you like it."

Tiana nodded, stealing a furtive look at Bayne. The eyes resting on her were smooth as jadestone and his face was set in an unreadable mask. Quickly, she averted her gaze.

"Why don't you relax and keep Peter company," Catherine suggested as she sliced a cucumber into a wooden salad bowl. "Dinner will be in about twenty minutes."

Although it had been done in the nicest possible way, Tiana knew she had been dismissed. She could take a hint! Besides, she wasn't at all sure she would have liked remaining in the kitchen, so near Bayne. Funny, how just that afternoon she had considered it such a large friendly room. Without a sound, Tiana returned to the living room.

Luckily, she found Peter in an oddly quiet mood. He was still preoccupied with his equipment and Tiana found a magazine before sitting down. She wanted no more of Peter's perceptive insights and so she was content to page through a magazine she didn't care to read.

Once they were all seated around the dinner table Peter's absorption evaporated. He made a conscientious effort to join in the conversation as did everyone. Since her earlier silence had been noted by Peter, Tiana overcame her reserve and joined in as they talked about current events and several new films.

Near the end of the meal, Peter informed Tiana he would be taking some night shots of her by the ravine he and Catherine had found earlier. Tiana accepted the assignment, privately rejoicing in being spared extended contact with Bayne. Catherine asked to come with them, and for one teetering second Tiana thought Bayne might come. But no, he said he could use the time to do paperwork.

By the time Tiana had changed into her elf costume and donned a windbreaker, Bayne was nowhere to be seen. Armed with high-intensity flashlights, the trio set off for the dry gully. Coolness was kicking its lively heels in the night air and Tiana jammed one hand into the pocket of the windbreaker. The jacket repelled the wind but did little to thwart the chilling cold.

When they reached the location, Peter was once again the demanding professional. His brusque direction soon eliminated any impulse Tiana may have unwittingly entertained of enjoying the experience. His compatriot was the nippy wind cutting through her thin costume until she found it altogether quite unpleasant.

Gritting her teeth, Tiana followed Peter's direction by climbing within the rim of the crevice. Regardless of everything that had happened, she was determined to make this trip worthwhile. Although it had been a personal disaster, she vowed to salvage what she could of the original purpose of coming to Connecticut. Tiana concentrated on the task at hand—after all, she was here to model. So, she dutifully arched her body, smiled, did not smile, and did numerous other things to carry out Peter's directions. It was a commendable effort on her part but when Peter finally called a halt, Tiana showed more than a little relief.

The night had grown steadily colder and even when Tiana put her windbreaker back on, it did not help. The three of them walked back to the house in a brisk stride that did not encourage talk. Tiana was in the lead as they reached the back porch. She pushed open the door and came face to face with Bayne in the act of pouring a cup of coffee. The motion was arrested as his eyes sought and found hers. It was an immutable tableau of such soul-destroying poignancy, neither seemed capable of speech.

But the other two caught up with Tiana and were impatiently waiting to enter the kitchen. And as time often does, the moment slid away. The stirring mosaic they had created was shattered, the bits and pieces flung aside.

"Coffee!" The word was a joyous celebration from Catherine as she dropped her camera and other paraphernalia on the table. She rubbed her hands together. "It's cold out there!"

"Here." Bayne finished pouring and passed her the cup.

Catherine took a sip from the steaming mug. "Ah, nice and hot."

Peter's equipment joined Catherine's on the table. "Any more coffee?"

Bayne had gotten down three more cups and was pouring into one of them. "Plenty! Tiana?"

"Please," she answered.

All four of them sat around the table drinking coffee and conversing. Actually, Peter did most of the talking, telling Bayne about the relative failure of the night's picture-taking session. He was careful to say he would not know for certain until the film was developed but it did not relieve Tiana of her sense of failure. Peter had still not gotten the one special shot he wanted so desperately.

Soon after finishing his cup of coffee, Peter got to his feet. "I think I'll turn in now. I have work to do in the morning and so does Tiana. Coming?" He glanced meaningfully at Tiana.

But he needn't have bothered, because she was already draining the last of the coffee from her cup. She had no intention of being the unwelcomed third party. "Yes." She hastily rose to her feet.

They both washed their cups and set them to dry before saying good night. As Tiana passed in front of Peter to go to the door, he hooked an affable arm over her shoulder. He kept it there until they reached her bedroom. Then he turned her to face him, his hand cupping her shoulder. "I'll call you first thing in the morning. I want to get some shots at Look-Out-Point. You don't mind, do you?"

"Are you giving me a choice?" The black line of her eyebrow quirked wryly.

"Nope!" Peter had the unmitigated nerve to grin shamelessly as he gave her hair a tug. Before she could retaliate, he was down the hall, whistling a jaunty tune.

Tiana stood there a moment watching him as she shook her head in disbelief. It never ceased to amaze her how one individual, so casual and unassuming in his appearance, could maneuver people so unconcernedly. The odd part was, they rarely seemed to mind. Occasionally Peter might annoy her, but he never threatened her peace of mind. That distinction belonged to a disturbing auburn-headed man with capti vating green eyes. He was the man who sent her pulse racing and a fire lapping through her veins even while her mind recognized the folly of it.

The seemingly utter and total quiet of the country actually had a breathing, teeming life of its own. The night sounds murmured together in a sighing hush and without the omnipresent lights of the city, the blackness was almost palatable. When a softly persistent voice intruded on Tiana's slumber, she pulled the blanket over her head and scrunched down further in the comforting warmth of the bed.

Again, it came. "Tiana! Come on! It's time to get up!"

Even though the layers of covers distorted the voice, she nevertheless recognized it as Peter's. Striving to ignore the unwanted call, Tiana burrowed deeper, her sleep-drugged senses refusing to believe it was time to awake.

"Rise and shine! Come on! Get a move on!"

She mumbled incoherently and responded by pulling the pillow over her head. The blanket had simply not done the job! The pillow though did blunt the encroaching sound of his uninvited voice.

But alas, he would not take the hint! The next thing she knew, the blanket was twitched aside and a blast of cool air played frigidly over her body. With a labored effort, Tiana rolled to her side, pushing up a section of the pillow so she could peer out. Prying her eyes open, she saw it was still dark. The discovery produced her first question. "What time is it?"

"Not quite five," he answered in a spurious whisper.

"Oh, no!" Tiana croaked in a sleep crusted voice. She threw herself back on her stomach, anchoring the pillow firmly with her hands on both sides.

Peter wrestled the pillow from her and tossed it

unceremoniously to the foot of the bed along with the booty of blankets. "Come on! Up and at-em!"

She groaned as if in real physical pain. "Why do we have to go out while it's still dark?"

"Because I want to get some pictures of you against the dawn. So you have to get up the rock formation before the first light. Get yourself together and I'll put some coffee on. If you hurry you can have a cup." As he opened the door to leave, his parting shot was, "Fifteen minutes, no more."

Ever so reluctantly, Tiana unwound her body after she heard the door close. She blindly reached for the bedside lamp and clicked it on. Squinting into the unrelenting light, she pushed her feet over the side of the bed to the floor. Annoyance flared briefly when she heard Peter's muffled chuckle from the hallway. Obviously, he had not completely trusted her to carry out his orders.

She was usually very conscientious about obeying Peter's wishes, however it was more than thirty minutes before she joined him in the kitchen. It took most of that time to dress and to do her hair and makeup, but she was determined not to be rushed. After Peter had chuckled, Tiana had glanced at the clock and discovered it was not even four o'clock, in fact it was barely after three. Peter had not been altogether honest in his estimation of the time when he had told her it was not yet five.

Unperturbed by her tardiness, Peter poured her a steaming cup of coffee. He had another one himself while she drank hers. However, his consideration stopped short of allowing her a second cup. Peter ended any thought she might have had about a refill by jumping to his feet the moment she finished sipping. When he grabbed his equipment from the table, a strap tangled with the top of one of the ladder-back chairs.

As he tried to unsnarl it, the chair tipped over and crashed to the floor. In the foredawn quiet, it sounded much louder than it had any right to sound. He leaned over to pick it up, apologizing shamefacedly before ordering, "Let's go!"

Dawn had not broken when they reached the rise below Look-Out-Point. Peter remained guardedly at the base of the projection, holding the flashlights while Tiana scaled the boulders. The day before, Bayne had chosen a way marked by footholds but in the inky darkness, Tiana could not locate all of them. She should have paid closer attention but then yesterday her thoughts had been focused elsewhere. Tiana supposed glumly, she only had herself to blame. Finally Peter called up for her to stop on one particularly dramatic boulder jutting out from a plateau. She positioned herself under Peter's guidance long before the first streaky rays of light appeared across the eastern sky.

After a short span of disorientation, Tiana found she liked working at this elevation in the dark. She experienced such an immense feeling of freedom, it could only be compared with the feeling that sometimes overcame her when she was engrossed in painting. Except for the verbal directions of the photographer, she could have been completely alone. Even the recurring sighs of the camera, so far below, failed to unbalance her new-found sense of creative liberation.

Gradually the morning light began to whittle away the night. The world became a kaleidoscope of changing shadows. From deepest indigo to the palest silver, the light brushed the earth and stroked the surrounding landscape.

"The sun is about to break behind you! Climb on that top rock," Peter hollered.

"All right." The next level was over her head, so

Tiana lodged a foot in a ragged indentation in the obdurate surface of the boulder to give herself a leg up. She heard a stifled admonition to be careful but did not stop until she was standing. She gleaned the shifting shadows below. "Okay, now what?"

"Get back, you fool!" Bayne's voice pierced the air with chilly restraint.

Although shaken from the unexpectedness of his presence, Tiana immediately back-stepped from the lip of the rock. Even as she did, her eyes sifted the distance in a concerted effort to see him. Bayne moved from the base of the formation and she could distinguish his uniquely male silhouette. The artist's memory in her recalled his face in minute detail, every bold angle and curving line, even though her eyes could not differentiate the features. The mere remembrance ignited the old flooding warmth and soon every cell in her body was awash with tingling awareness. Bayne stood below, his hands on his hips, feet planted apart, head lifted high; and she could not take her eyes from him.

Tiana was unaware of the indulgent monologue of Peter's camera but she knew the split second Bayne chose to step further from the outcropping lessening the angle between them. Now she perceived him as real and not as some mythical entity conjured by her starved imagination. Her heart took one wild, soaring leap as she heard him say to Peter, "Are you crazy putting her up there?"

The thought of Bayne being worried about her personal safety sent a molten liquid racing through her veins, but just as quickly his next words iced not only the streaming fire but her heart as well.

"Have you forgotten Tiana is the girl who nearly broke her neck falling off your ladder? And only yesterday afternoon, she turned an ankle coming off a three foot high wall! Now you put her up there without even a safety wire! You'll never get the picture you want if she falls!" Bayne's sonorous voice vibrated with seething anger.

Bayne made no attempt to lower his voice, no attempt to save her pride. Never before had he indicated he thought she was clumsy. But as he dredged up those old accidents, Tiana was left in little doubt about his impressions of her. Here was another fault he added to the growing list of her discernible shortcomings. He was only concerned because if she fell, Peter would not get his precious picture and then Bayne might lose the Avery account. Bayne didn't care about her safety! He only cared about the danger to the campaign if she were hurt. Peter made some sort of reply but Tiana could not hear what it was. Peter never told her to move so Tiana stood right where she was and his camera continued its relentless pursuit.

Her eyes culled the thinning darkness, but it was more than darkness that separated her from Bayne. It was the knowledge that he had belittled her. It was bad enough to insult her to her face but to talk like he had to Peter was unforgivable. She watched with pained interest as Bayne moved back to the base of the projection. She dully noted his climb to the first level and his wait there. Seconds ticked by like never-ending hours as Bayne displayed the instinctive patience of a hawk studying its prey: intense, watchful, motionless.

After a decided gap of time, Peter called, "You can come down. I've got what I was after!"

Ignoring the jubilation in Peter's announcement, Tiana shivered as she glanced over her shoulder, wishing there was a way down in that direction. Unfortunately, for her, it was a sheer, deadly drop. She had to climb down the way she had come up—the way now marked by Bayne. Lowering herself to her stomach, Tiana wriggled over the side of the boulder. Her feet dangled uncomfortably in space as she frantically searched for a toe-hold. When she had just about given up hope of ever finding it, she felt a strong hand close over her foot, forcefully shoving it into a crevice. Bayne reached for her waist but she did not need his help now that she had her foot in the natural rock shelf. She did not want his help. It reminded her too vividly of those other times when he had been collecting impressions of her clumsiness. She would not give him the satisfaction of yet another piece of misconstrued evidence on which to build his defamatory case against her.

As Tiana made the drop to his level, she jerked away from him. The violence of her move did not completely free her from his touch. All it succeeded in doing was to cause her to brush against the roughened surface of the rock with such uncontrolled force that she tore the leg of her costume. It was an irreparable rend! She stared at the gaping hole and then at Bayne. Expectedly she saw the nerveless impatience stamped on the granite features of his face.

For one insane instant she wanted to pound her fists into his chest, to beat out her frustration, to put the blame on him for her ripped costume, to make him suffer as she was suffering. But, of course, she did not. Sanity returned, bringing with it a desire to scurry away from him to some distant corner of the world; but there would be no corner, no place, no sanctuary out of his reach. Destined to love him, she faced the truth that he would never return it. Bleakness brimmed in her eyes. Would she forever be condemned to this torture that had become her life? Forever wanting a man she could not have. For more reasons than there are stars in the sky, Tiana had to get away from him.

He sighed but his eyes did not leave her face. Then in a voice as enticing as satin, he asked, "Won't you let me help you?"

"No!" she cried the word through silent lips. Her voice died in the stricture of her throat as she sought to swallow the rising grief. Desperately, she shook her head.

"Tiana, you don't mean it." It was subdued, lulling.

"I do!" she reiterated through narrowed lips. "How many times do I have to tell you that I don't need you? If I needed help I would have called Peter."

The small scar whitened in the early morning light and grainy shafts spearheaded the anger in his eyes. She had broken through his veneer of gentleness. "Peter? Do you seriously think he has the sensitivity to know when you need help?"

"He has more understanding than you'll ever have." She met his anger with some of her own, unknowingly bringing with it taintless sincerity.

"I suppose you consider yourself to be an astute judge of people and human nature?" he said in derision, uncaring of the hurt he was inflicting.

She glared at him. "I form my own opinions of people, if that's what you mean. I don't befriend someone simply because it's socially or economically expedient to do so!"

"Oh, that's rich coming from someone who mirrors everything that crosses her path, from someone incapable of making a clear-headed objective judgement," he bit out harshly.

His scorching accusations hurled past her defenses. Mirror? What did he mean? Did he see the love she had for him? Or did he think she reacted to all men the way she did to him? One thought was as abhorrent as the other. She stopped breathing. "What are you saying?"

"You may form your own opinions about people but with your unbridled idealism, how much of a variance is there? In addition to that, anyone with a little experience could read the way you think simply by looking at your face."

Tiana breathed out in relief. Bayne was grinding his axe against the same old stone—her idealism. As long as he had not guessed about her love for him she could deal with the other. "That does not even deserve an answer." She put a frosty edge to it.

"Which translates to: There is no defense because you know I'm right!" he sneered.

"No, it doesn't! I'm sick and tired of arguing with you!" she flared.

Bayne stared at her, incredulity sharpening his knifing gaze. He watched as she lifted her chin, scrutinizing her with his glittering green eyes. And then a strange thing happened! His eyes shut briefly and when they opened the white-hot surge of anger had drained away. He refused the challenge.

Tiana thought she must be mistaken. His anger couldn't have faded so abruptly. She blinked and when he again imprisoned her eyes, she was sure. The anger was gone! And in its place was a new kind of macabre humor: cold, calculating, cynical. She did not know its source nor its cause and she could not even gage its significance but terror shot through her limbs turning them to jelly.

"Hey! Are you two going to be up there all day?" Peter shouted.

"Are we?" There was mockery in his whisper, unconcealed scorn meant only for her ears.

Her mouth tightened. She shook her head as speech eluded her. She prayed for strength to return to her legs.

"Will you go first or shall I?" His brow lifted with disdain.

She wished her mind could form a taunt to throw in his arrogant face, but he surpassed her by eons in experience. So she had to satisfy herself with, "If you go first, I'll follow. Then I'll be able to see where to put my feet." She made the admission and was amazed to see how little it cost.

"We're coming." Bayne called down to Peter. Then he bowed his head in acknowledgement to Tiana.

He helped her down the formation, as they both knew he would. But he only touched her when absolutely necessary and then with a detachment that surprised her. Not one word was exchanged on the climb down nor for that matter, on the hike back to the house. The pattern was set for the day. Although they remained in Connecticut until late in the afternoon, the easy congeniality of the day before was never harnessed. Tiana and Bayne could have been two strangers trapped together; the politeness forced and stiff between them.

Chapter Eight

During the following week, Tiana could honestly admit that she was glad to be on leave from the Dahlquist Agency. It would have been expecting too much to see Bayne daily and not respond in some extreme way to him. However she needed more than physical distance to eradicate his image from her thoughts. Still, in unguarded moments, her mind clung tenaciously to remembrances of him; words spoken, looks given, and every enduring action of his. As loathe as Tiana was to face it, she knew her only hope lay in the salvation of time. Elongated stretches of it would be necessary to wean her from the domination of her unrequited love. The pain and frustration of attempting to diminish her feeling for Bayne were as sharp and unrelenting as anything Tiana had encountered in the whole of her life.

However, one small anguish was spared her. Catherine Hunter had flown to California on Monday for a modeling assignment and had decided to take a vacation in Hawaii. She would be gone at least another two weeks and Tiana could not help but be relieved. Catherine was always so empathetic and understanding, never issuing a condemnation of Tiana's behavior. It intensified Tiana's guilt even more than might have been the case had her roommate not been such a paragon.

The activity and pace of the last week was mild in comparison to the frenzy of the preceding weeks. And for the first time in ages, Tiana had time to paint. In fact, she had spent most of the day in her SoHo studio. And when daylight faded, she stopped off at a Russian restaurant for dinner before returning to her apartment across from Central Park. She thought of telephoning her parents but remembered they were still in Europe, having volunteered as chaperons for a student tour.

She found her apartment too quiet, too conducive to images better left unformed. In an unusual fit of restlessness, Tiana put some records on the stereo, deliberately choosing spirited, up-beat selections designed to keep her from succumbing to the hovering moodiness. Back and forth, she paced in front of the window, disinterestedly noting the few hardy souls braving the park at night. Then her gaze flitted down to study the figures disappearing under the massive canopy at the entrance of her building. When the doorbell chimed, she fairly skipped to answer it. The doorman had not paged her, so she knew it had to be either a neighbor or else someone exceedingly well known to him.

Happy for the company, Tiana yanked open the door and found Peter there. He was barely able to restrain a vibrant excitement. He clutched a thin leather carrying case under his arm as he bounded through the foyer into the living room. His gait was a bouncing step Tiana had seen only once before—the day he had told her about the Elfin Magic contract.

One of her black eyebrows lifted as she watched Peter fling himself on the couch. He shoved aside a decorative crystal bowl from its usual place on the coffee table and staked out an area for the leather case.

Pulling a flat folder from it, he ordered impatiently, "Hurry up! I have something to show you!"

Interest aroused, Tiana dutifully slipped into the seat next to him. She schooled her expression to one of alert receptiveness in order to hide the fond smile about to capture her mouth.

Peter flexed his arms and rotated his wrists with a flourish as a demented light glimmered in his eyes. He cocked his head in her direction. "Ready?"

"Yes," Tiana said dryly, wondering what had gotten him so revved up.

And then in the next blinding instant, she knew. He flicked open the top of the folder to reveal the layout of the Elfin Magic advertisement. She did not need Peter or anyone else to tell her this was the picture—the print ad—that would be reproduced on magazine pages throughout the world. Tiana had to force herself to look at it, not to flinch away.

Four-fifths of the page was covered with a full-length photograph of Tiana in her elf costume. At the bottom was a tiny picture of Elfin Magic cologne. Next to it was scripted the caption:

The only other magic a woman will ever want!

Her eyes scarcely skimmed the copy before being drawn again to her picture. The shadowy light and the muted grey surface beneath her feet told her quicker than any words where this particular picture had been taken. It had been shot early in the morning at Look-Out-Point, when she first discovered Bayne's presence. Studying the ad she intuitively knew Peter had captured that moment when love had touched her features. So the weekend was not a total loss, after all. Even from the acrid ashes of her love, a phoenix could rise.

"Well?" Peter was delightedly expectant.

"I don't know what to say." Tiana finally tore her eyes away from the picture to glance at Peter.

"You could tell me it's good, no, make it great!" His joyful enthusiasm knew no limits.

"You know it is," Tiana rejoined evenly, feeling none of his overriding excitement, only a gnawing ache inside her middle. "It's one of those you took last weekend, isn't it?"

"It sure is and it's even better than I dared hope! Just look at this baby!" He plucked the ad up and waved it in front of her. "This is perfect! It appeals to both men and women. This . . ." He beat a drumroll with his fingertips against the picture. ". . . is how a woman in love is—desirous and just a little fearful." His gaze ferried from the ad to Tiana. "Hey! What's the matter? Are you ill or something?" Furrows of concern marked Peter's brow.

"Or something," she answered lifelessly as she swallowed back the erupting sickness within her.

"We're friends! You can tell me what's bothering you. Don't you like the ad?"

Peter sounded so genuinely interested that Tiana's eyes crawled back to him from the unfocused point in space. A shuddering sigh escaped, taking with it some of the fierce pain. Her gaze beseeched him. "I don't suppose there is any chance of not using the picture?"

"Are you out of your mind?" Peter's head reared back. "No way! This is literally one picture in a million! Why wouldn't you want them to print it?"

Tiana compressed her lips. "In the picture, I look so . . . so . . . oh, I don't know." Her hands fluttered as she tried unsuccessfully to describe it.

The corners of Peter's eyes turned down as his gaze tightened on her. "The look on the face of the woman in this ad speaks of enchantment and an effortless beauty derived from her love. What's wrong with that?"

As he said what Tiana feared hearing the most, her breathing halted. Dumbly, she shook her head, knowing the whitened mask of composure on her face could crack at any moment to reveal the tension and strain concealed beneath.

"That's it?" Peter made the deduction in obvious disbelief. "All this is because I caught a picture of you looking like a woman in love?"

Her teeth gouged the flesh of her lip. "Yes."

"Why?" It was more than a question; it was a command.

Lifting her shoulders, Tiana's eyes left him to bounce disinterestedly around the room. Anything was better than facing him—the Grand Inquisitor.

"Does it have to do with the way you feel about Bayne?" Peter asked.

It was out! Her gaze flew to Peter, confirming the truth.

Peter's eyes widened perceptively. "So what? I know how you feel about Bayne but I would never say anything, if that's what is bothering you."

She was touched by his loyalty. But of course, that was not what was worrying her. "Thank you, Peter, but that's not the problem."

"You'll have to explain yourself," he declared, none-too-gently.

"All right." Tiana owed him an explanation. "If you know how I feel, then so will everyone else—so will Bayne."

"I see-e-e." The words were drawn out into a hum. "Tiana, I think I should point out that your logic is all fouled up. First of all, I've had a front row seat to everything going on between you and Bayne. To put it another way, I think I've probably seen the two of you together more than anyone else. Believe me when I tell you, it took me quite a while to figure out how you felt about him, and in the second place, models work in illusion. I know you don't think of yourself as a model, but other people do and they will assume you deliberately created the look for the camera."

Peter's attempt to lighten her oppressive burden rebounded off the wall of her self-pity. "Aren't you forgetting Bayne?"

"What does he have to do with it?" Then Peter's eyes opened even more as he answered his own question. "You haven't told Bayne how you feel about him and you think he will know when he sees this picture!"

Avoiding Peter's eyes, she nodded her head with reluctance.

"Bayne has already seen the ad and he thought it was a good one. He is used to dealing with models and knows only too well their abilities. It never crossed his mind that the look in the photograph had any basis in reality. He figured it for a pose."

"Are you sure?" she asked doubt-riddenly.

"Hey! I'm as sure as anyone can be about anything in this world of ours. Nothing in life comes with a guarantee." The palms of his hands were extended upwards.

Sadly, she nodded, wishing it could be otherwise.

"There is one thing I don't understand. Why don't you want Bayne to know how you feel?" Peter stated bluntly, not softening the blow.

"Oh Peter, there is a lot you don't know."

"Granted!" he said flippantly, his eyes rolling up.

She winced. "Bayne doesn't even want me around. He told me to go back to Georgia and said I didn't belong here." Even after all this time, the remembrance still tugged wildly at her feelings.

"It doesn't sound like something Bayne would say," Peter observed. "When did he tell you that?"

"The day you hired me for your assistant."

Laughingly, Peter rejoined, "Be reasonable, Tiana! How can you hold something he might have said at an initial meeting against him now?"

"Not might have said, he did say it!" she argued, ridiculously setting her focus adrift.

"Okay-okay, so he did say it," Peter conceded. "Has Bayne said anything similar since then?"

The edge of her lower lip curled under. "No, I don't think so, but only because he needed me for the Elfin Magic campaign."

"Aw, Tiana, be serious!" Peter hooted. "Bayne didn't need you for the campaign. If he didn't want you around, he would have gotten someone else."

"You said there wasn't anyone else." She stared at him, accusation glistening like starfire in her eyes.

With a cheeky grin, Peter confessed, "Listen, I would have told you the earth was flat and the moon was a giant Frisbee, if I thought it would have influenced you to sign the contract. It was my idea to use you and I sold the Averys on it."

Hurt and indignation warred for possession of her face. "How could you? I trusted you, Peter! I believed you!" Oh, she had been so gullible, letting him lead her down the garden path without a murmur of protest.

"Everyone benefited from what I did, including you, Tiana. I doubt your option will be picked up but you will still get a tidy figure for a one-year obligation. You have nothing to complain about on that score. You have money in the bank, a secured job at the agency and a range of contacts and opportunities you wouldn't have otherwise."

"I suppose so," she voiced half-heartedly, knowing he was right but stubbornly feeling betrayed.

"And if you're still concerned about the ad, don't be. Remember, I'm the only one who knows that the look in the ad is only visible on your face when Bayne is near you."

Her brow puckered. "I don't understand."

"Well, I was puzzled at first too, until it struck me that only the pictures I took when Bayne was in the room had the charismatic spark I was aiming for in the Elfin pictures. Alone, your pictures showed a pretty girl but when Bayne was around, they revealed a young woman crossing the bridge to womanhood. On the one side was her innocence and childhood and on the unexplored side was the promise of fulfillment and knowledge." Peter relaxed against the back of the couch, his hands threaded behind his neck. "Now thinking about it, I must have seen the possibility on the day I hired you."

"I don't believe you!" Tiana stated forthrightly.

"Not when you first came into the office for the interview but later when I returned to find you talking with Bayne," Peter explained. "When I came back in the room, the seed must have been planted in my mind to use you in the Elfin campaign. Looking back, I'm sure I saw promise even then."

"Peter, I had just met Bayne! It couldn't have been love you saw." Tiana made a rare stab at pragmatic reasoning.

"Often the heart knows before the head," he chided in subdued amusement. "Besides I'm not swearing it's gospel, only saying it's what I recollect."

"By any chance, did you arrange the trip to Connecticut to test out your theory?" Her eyes trapped his.

"Right you are!" Peter chuckled. "But Bayne being Bayne almost spoiled my plans. I intended for him to come out to the ravine on Saturday night but he chose to remain behind. I didn't want to arouse any suspicions so I let it go. In a way it was too bad because I had this perfect vision of you rising from the earth. Anyway things worked out for the best. The shot of you on the boulders is well worth a bushel of thwarted plans."

Tiana smiled weakly, the corners of her mobile mouth wavering. "Everyone fell right in with your plans."

"Let's just say, I left very little to chance." His gaze sailed back to the ad. "There will never be another picture like this one!" His fingers caressed the edge of the layout with reverence.

"I should hope not!" The bitterness evaporated, leaving a bad taste in her mouth.

Peter laughed, "You poor thing! I wish there were something I could do. You've been through the wringer lately."

"Don't! Please don't!" she implored prosaically. "I don't think I can take any more of your help and survive untarnished."

"Tiana, be fair. What if I just said a word or two in the right place?"

"No!" There was a new firmness in her voice. "Leave well enough alone. Besides, Bayne and I are not even speaking."

"I noticed. You want to tell me about it?"

She shook her head. "It doesn't matter. But it's important that you won't say anything to Bayne about what we've talked about."

"Tiana, I love the way the ad turned out and I want you to be happy."

Sighing, Tiana said, "It's not in your power to make me happy, not the way you mean and not right now." She managed a faint smile.

"It's against my nature to leave it like this." But the calculating gleam springing into his eyes was definitely an integral part of him. "Let me give it some thought."

"Peter!" she said warningly.

His eyes argued with hers for a moment and then he changed the subject. "Now with this ad taken care of, I can go to Paris with a clean slate."

"I didn't know you were going to Paris. When do you leave?" Tiana had been so caught up in the Elfin Magic campaign and her feelings about Bayne that she had lost touch with other events.

"Saturday morning," he answered.

"Is it business or a vacation?" she inquired.

"Some of both, I guess," he equivocated. "I've scheduled three weeks over there so if everything goes according to plan, I should have time to relax."

"You are so lucky to be going to Paris! Have you ever been there?" She could not keep the note of envy from her voice.

"Sure, plenty of times," he responded casually as his eyes narrowed reflectively. "Haven't you ever been there?"

"No, but one day I intend to go. Way down deep, every artist hopes to have a chance to go to Paris. Maybe next year." She sighed wistfully.

After a rather pensive silence, Peter spoke. "Why not go this year? Why not with me?"

Confused Tiana stared at him. "With you?"

"Why not? Have you forgotten you are my assistant? Now with the Elfin campaign out of the way, there is no reason why you can't resume your duties. Anyway, it would pay you back in some small part for what this campaign of yours will do for my career."

"Oh, I couldn't do that." And yet even as she said the words, her eyes took on a warm glow.

Peter laughed, "Of course you can! There's nothing to stop you from coming with me."

"Is it really possible?"

"It's more than possible. You're going and that's all there is to it," Peter ordered.

"Only if you're sure it would be all right," she qualified.

"Nothing to it. It's no big deal," he responded offhandedly.

"Maybe not to you it isn't. But I would rather go to Paris than anything else in the world." Just the thought of the galleries and museums brought a smile to her lips.

"You don't mean it," he challenged. "Wouldn't you rather have Bayne than a trip to Paris?"

The clarity of her eyes misted and the smile dimmed. "Realistically speaking, this trip is the best I can hope for now."

"Humm, we'll see . . ."

"Peter!" she warned seriously, far from smiling.

"All right, all right!" His hand came up to deflect her objections. "Before I forget, do you have a valid passport?"

"No." Fear crawled into her voice.

"Not to worry. It usually takes about two weeks but I have a contact who can rush it through." His eyes left her to return to the layout. Carefully he slipped it into the carrying case and a short while later he left.

After Peter's departure, Tiana was no longer at loose ends nor was she unduly disturbed about the picture for the ad. Thoughts of Paris flitted in and out of her mind like glorious sunbeams through grey clouds. Perhaps after three weeks in Paris, Tiana would return to New York less in love with Bayne.

Chapter Nine

A suitcase lay open on the floor of Tiana's bedroom as she stood at her closet methodically rooting through the contents. Occasionally, she paused to consider one garment or another more closely, but for the most part, left them where they hung. This was the last chore on a long list of items she had to get done before leaving for Paris in the morning. As if she had been under the watchful eye of a friendly genie, Tiana had actually managed to accomplish everything but the packing of her clothes. There had been a scary moment when she thought her passport might not be secured in time, but Peter made a telephone call and the precious document now rested on the top of her bureau. She could hardly believe she would be flying to Paris, France, in the morning!

The doorbell chimed, sending her flying through the apartment to answer it. She half expected it to be Peter. Tiana had talked to him earlier and Peter mentioned he might be coming over. A ready smile formed as she adjusted the long folds of her blue robe and secured the sash before pulling open the door.

It was *not* Peter!

Bayne's eyes narrowed to razor slits, fragmenting her

molded happiness into thousands of misplaced emotions. "Tiana, may I come in?"

"Catherine is still in Hawaii." She stood frozen to the spot. Bayne was here to see Catherine, wasn't he?

"I know."

He knew Catherine had not returned from her trip! Tiana back-stepped, allowing him to enter and then with growing nervousness, she followed him into the living room. Self-consciously, she offered him a drink and a chair, but he refused both. Instead he chose to walk the length of the room, his hands clasped behind his back. Tiana was forced to sit down, positively doubting her ability to remain standing in his presence on legs that were swiftly turning to water. Mystified, her eyes tracked him as his athletic stride carried him to the windows. He looked out through the glass as if he had forgotten her. Then just as suddenly as he had begun pacing, Bayne pivoted and strode back to her. His striking gaze glimmered with an unrecognizable light over her upturned face.

Bayne thrust a hand into the side pocket of his brown slacks and the unmistakable outline of a male fist could be seen under the tautened material. "Peter stopped by my office today to clear his travel voucher and leave a copy of his itinerary. I found out he intends to take you with him."

Tiana stiffened. She could feel the wrath building ominously within Bayne, a barely surpressible fury that threatened to be unleashed at any moment. If there was any chance to avoid it, now was the time. "I'm going with him. But if there is any problem about expenses, I'll pay my own."

He frowned distractedly. "I'm not concerned about your misguided Puritan ethic. I don't care who pays for your ticket. I came to find out if you're really going through with it."

"Why shouldn't I go?" Defensiveness streaked out of her.

"Why indeed!" A muscle tensed along his jawline hardening the grave features of his face. "Is this your solution to what happened in Connecticut?"

"Nothing happened." She sought a level of flat denial but somehow her voice caught and the words were utterly strained.

"Only because you refused to talk about it like an adult," Bayne scowled.

Now she saw clearly what was at the bottom of Bayne's unannounced visit. Well, Tiana had no desire to discuss her feelings. "As far as I'm concerned, there is nothing to say."

"Quiet!" he scythed through her objection. "I know Peter has been a great help getting your modeling career started, but do you have any idea where your relationship with him will end?"

"I won't discuss Peter with you." Alarm primed her declaration. When Bayne mentioned Peter's name, Tiana got a jumpy feeling, as if the whole house of cards built on the secret of her love would come tumbling down.

"Precisely the way I feel! There is no need to discuss anyone else. It is my preference to talk about us."

Bayne had thrown a curve ball. Tiana had not expected him to say that nor had she expected to see the remembered half smile on his mouth. Her heart began to pound and she wished it wouldn't. She desperately needed all her energies to focus on what he was saying.

"Suppose you start by telling me why you're going to Paris," he commanded unblinkingly as his mouth evened to an uncompromising line.

Relief slowed her thundering heart beat. At least, he had asked her an easy question. "I've always dreamed

of going to Paris. I've never known an artist who hasn't.
I'll spend every free moment in the galleries and
museums."

He sighed so deeply, so unreservedly, he seemed
to be digging into a forgotten well of patience. "I
thought as much when Peter told me you were going.
Do you have any idea of the significance of traveling with Peter? Do you know why he is taking you?
Why any man takes a woman on a jaunt to Europe?"

It was as if Bayne had thrown a glass of ice water in
her face. Tiana did not miss the vile accusation, the
brutal slur. "It's not like you think! Peter is taking
me . . . is taking me because . . ." she stopped abruptly. She could not tell Bayne the reason for the trip. She
couldn't!

"Yes?" he prompted with thinning tolerance.

"Because he thought I should get away for a while."
A slight tremor took her voice.

"Exactly! He wants you to get away all right. Get
away from the competition, so he can have you all to
himself."

Flinging her head from side to side, Tiana endeav-
ored to shake off the nightmarish effect of his words.
"No-no! You have it all wrong! It's not like that with
Peter!"

With a disgruntled sound, Bayne's eyes slashed
across her stricken face. "When did he offer to take you
to Paris?"

Her agitated movement ceased as she settled confused eyes on him. But her voice would not obey her
and no words would come to her lips.

"Wasn't it after you wrapped up the Elfin Magic
ad?" he prodded confidently. Something in her face
must have given him the answer for Bayne charged,
"Just as I thought!"

Spurred to action by his scathing contempt, Tiana cried, "It's not what you think!"

"If it isn't now it certainly will be by the time you return from Paris. Haven't you learned anything at all about Peter? Manipulation is second nature to him. He could be the reincarnation of Machiavelli! He does nothing without a motive!"

No! She did not believe what Bayne said and yet how could she defend Peter without revealing to Bayne the whole truth? Unshed tears gathered in her eyes, put there by a bedeviling array of emotions. She tried to blink them away but the image of Bayne remained a blurred watercolor before her swimming vision.

"Tears, Tiana?" His voice softened.

Her gaze clung to him as a sob shuddered through her.

"Your tears could move Satan to compassion. Do you know that, Tiana?"

"Satan, but not you!" The words were garbled but the thought was clear.

"Ah Tiana, you are wrong, so very wrong. Despite my best intentions not to interfere, I'm here. I do care and I came to try one last time." He reached down for her hands and pulled her unresistingly to her feet.

One rebellious tear was dislodged to slip past the barrier of her lashes. It slowly trickled down her cheek. Gently, with one finger, Bayne wiped away her tear. "Don't cry. I never meant for you to cry." His arms circled her. "Sh-sh," he crooned.

With her head pillowed against his shoulder, there was no reason for Tiana to weep. "Bayne?" It was an aching call, husky from raw emotion.

He answered with his lips. They met hers with a tentative tasting and then with a supreme domination as her response was sparked. There would be no interruptions, no running away this time as she surrendered to the mastery of his embrace. Tiana was his as surely as the stars belong to the sky and the tides are part of the changing seas.

And when he took his mouth from hers, green eyes treasured her. "Tiana?" In her name was a question only her heart could decode.

She needed no other words for her heart had always known its answer even before there had been a question. It shone in the glow of her eyes before her lips mouthed "Yes."

Bayne picked her up in his arms and once more stole her breath with his mouth. Of their own accord, her arms wrapped themselves around his neck as her fingers were laced in his thick hair. He carried her to her bedroom, closing the door and stepping over the opened suitcase with an unhesitating tread. He lowered her to the bed, his own body joining hers in an expression of passion.

In a stranger's voice, Tiana murmured his name. It was a wingless plea unknowingly seeking an anchor.

His reply, given in the moist cavern of her mouth, was a sound vibrating within her body down to her toes and back again in sweet torture. Melding together, he repeated her name in a need-roughened whisper against her lips.

When he pulled his mouth from hers, Bayne blazed a fiery trail over her ears and down the sensitive, pulsing cord in her neck, bringing her nearer and nearer to the honeyed agony which was his alone to give. His mouth traveled to the point of the vee made by her robe, and there in the valley between her breasts the last hindrance was met and conquered. Expertly his fingers loosened the sash and flicked aside the only thing keeping her naked body from him. The warm light in his eyes and then the stroking of his hands immediately covered what had so recently been exposed.

His face was buried in the curve of her neck as his hands began a seductive journey over her assenting body. In a thickened voice, Bayne confessed, "After tonight, I swear you will be as obsessed with me as I am with you. You're a black-haired witch, who has driven me past all rational thought. I never wanted a woman as much as I've wanted you."

Wanted! Bayne only *wanted* her! Missing were the words of love! Nothing had changed. Her love had blinded her to the glaring reality. Bayne wanted her, sought to possess her, but her love was too golden to be thrown away on mere lust.

Thrashing, Tiana broke away from him to roll on her side, her back to him. With a superhuman effort she shook off the immediate effects of arousal. Rasping as pain intermingled with passion, she demanded, "What am I to you? A want?"

"You're a burning fire in my blood! You're a hunger within my flesh! Does that answer your question?" His hand curled around her shoulder, sliding off the silky robe. His mouth caressed her skin sending new electro-shocks of pleasure throbbing through her body. Inch by inch, his lips consumed her will.

"No! It's not enough!" Acting without volition, Tiana flung herself away from his touch, putting her back to the edge of the bed as she whipped the robe over her. As she stared at him from the far side of the double bed, her eyes pleaded with him, begged him to speak just one word of love, even if it were a lie.

He did not look at her. Bayne's body jack-knifed to a sitting position and then he took the other side of the bed as his. His feet hit the floor like an axe blade striking wood. He drove a hand through his hair. "There is a name for what you just did." At the quick indrawing of her breath, he glowered over his shoulder.

"I see you know what it is! Then it's about time you started taking responsibility for your own actions." His body twisted and his hands came down to haul her across the bed. When she was in the center of it, his arms imprisoned her, coming down on either side of her like bars on a cage.

The dark menace in his voice seeped through her, chilling her to the marrow. Unnatural fear nosed out passion for possession of her soul. She cowered away from him, sinking into the mattress.

"For heaven's sake, Tiana, I'm not going to attack you. So stop cringing like you've been beaten." His features were cast in harsh impenitent lines obliterating any tenderness that once might have been a part of him. "There are other ways of going about it."

Mortal terror edged out fear. Her hands came up to grasp his wrists as she tried to rip them from her sides. They would not budge! A silent cry dried in her throat. Tiana was an unwilling captive to a man past reason.

"I believe you said my desire for you wasn't enough," he stated with unparalleled coldness, seemingly unaware of her frantic struggle to gain her freedom. "All right, Tiana, I'm a businessman. You have something I want and I'll pay your price. Just name it."

A gasp was torn from her lips. Her hands lay motionless, no longer clawing at him. Too many encounters with this man told her of the undeniable existence of this cynical satyr. Bayne was offering to buy her like a commodity, as if her body were for sale like a common street . . . Her mind could go no further. It was too painful, too wretched a thought. Tiana had been on the verge of giving herself to him and Bayne had debased her gift by offering to pay for it.

In a choked whisper, she said, "You can't meet the

price." He would never pay the price of love. It was
beyond him to return her feeling because he did not
believe such things existed.

"I can get you anything you want," he snarled.

"What? Moonlight and roses? A yacht anchored off
the coast? A suite at the Plaza?" She threw back his
earlier taunts disdainfully. They had been bitterly aged
within her heart.

"My mistake." His lips curved with mockery. "Obviously you are worth much more. So what will it be? A
gallery of your own? Would you like to be the most
exclusive model in the world? Do you want financial
security? Tell me what it is you want!"

Tiana was past any tears now. Bayne had pushed her
past life itself. The brown eyes staring into his green
ones were as dead as the voice that spoke. "I'll tell you
what I want. Peace. I want you to go right now. How
many times must I tell you to leave me alone?"

"You won't have to tell me again!" His eyes bored
into her. Bayne snatched back his hands as if they had
been resting on a hot plate. The mattress protested as
he stood up. "You have made your choice! From now
on, you're on your own. But know this, after your trip
with Peter you won't have a job at my agency. You
have your contract with Elfin Magic and what you make
of it is your business . . . and Peter's." He wrenched
the door open and stood there as Tiana was frozen in
the glare of his hatred. "If there is any justice in the
world, I will never see you again."

He disappeared from her life much the way he had
first entered it; with no warning and with cataclysmic
results. He had gone without even bothering to survey
the carnage his words had wrought.

I will never see you again. His words were burned
into her brain until she knew nothing but the heartache
of their meaning. She had been marked for an early

death. To go on living in a world without Bayne would be an existence and not a life. She knew the ultimate despair when he severed the diaphanous thread between them. And when he walked out, Bayne had taken all her dreams with him, nothing remained but the memory.

Beyond tears, beyond the physical expression of grief, Tiana was consigned to a nameless hell. Sometime, long after Bayne had left, she called Peter's answering machine to leave a cryptic message saying her plans had changed and she would not be making the trip with him. Paris was another dream that no longer had any meaning. She would need solitude to suture the deep wound and make some plans for the future; a black future without hope.

When the first exploratory finger of daylight began to lift the darkness of night, the telephone rang, rousing her from the lifeless stupor long enough to register the sound. Tiana made no effort to answer it. Peter was probably calling her about the message and she could not bare the thought of talking to him or anyone. Like an injured creature who must go alone to lick its wound, Tiana pushed herself from the bed. Mechanically, she dressed, straightened the crumpled bedspread and shoved the empty suitcase into her closet. When she left the apartment building a short time later, she carried only her handbag. Where she was going, she would not need designer clothes.

The next weeks fused into a haze of frenzied painting. Tiana shut herself in her studio in SoHo, trying to exorcise the bleak demons within her by endless hours at the easel. She would stop only when she could not do otherwise; eating and sleeping only when her body could no longer function.

Putting a final stroke on the canvas before her, Tiana

deftly blended the color into the adjoining one. Then she stepped back to study the effect. With the wet brush still in her hand, Tiana pushed back the errant strand of hair slipping over her eye with her forearm. After abstractly dipping her brush into the mixture on her palette and carefully running the tapered bristles in tiny circles to pick up the desired pigment, she re-touched the brush to the picture. A knock came at the door. Grimacing, she left the painting. As she balanced the brush in the same hand as the palette, Tiana reached for the doorknob.

Bayne! Her mind silently screamed the name! Was she hallucinating? When his mouth lifted to an odd whimsy of a smile, she knew it was not her imagination. His eyes, faintly contemplative, were at variance with the glimmer of even teeth as his smile broadened.

Ridiculously, Tiana's hands began to tremble. The brush could be seen waving in the air. She tightened her grip to stave off the nervous movement and watched in mute horror as the brush slipped from her fingers to fall to the floor. She stared down at the blob of paint staining the floor as if she did not know what it was or how on earth it had gotten there. Foolishly, she wanted to cry. It was such a little accident, paint on the floor. Why should tears form now when they had evaded her for weeks?

Bayne made a sound that crossed over from annoy-ance to concern as he bent to pick up the brush. Standing once again, he took the palette from her. "May I come in?"

The humbleness of his request sent her eyes to his. Under the quietude of his gaze, she yielded and allowed him to enter. Even as she closed the door, Tiana had to retain the soundless sobs wracking her body.

"Tiana?" It was suspended between them like the

filmy specter of the past. He placed the brush and palette on a table, never taking his eyes from her.

In the old habit they had, her eyes locked with his. The acid taste of remembrance dried her tears and formed a solid shield of ice between them.

Measuring her, his gaze dulled as he sensed her reaction. He thrust a hand into the inner pocket of his jacket and extracted a white envelope and extended it to her. "I brought you something."

She could not bring herself to take it from him. What manner of refined torture was this, so cruel he would break his vow of never seeing her again?

He lowered his hand. "Would you rather I tell you about it?"

"Whatever," she replied without expression.

"It says," he tapped the edge of the envelope against the palm of his other hand, "our publishing client accepted the sketches you submitted. In fact, Asgard liked them so much, they want you to do all the art-work for the campaign. The original budget has been beefed-up so it is now a major contract." He drew a breath. "Naturally I told them you no longer worked for us. So they are willing to commission you on a free-lance basis or to sign you to their own payroll."

The irony of it did not escape Tiana. She had achieved her dream of becoming a commercial artist when the dream had already died. Bayne had once predicted all her illusions would disappear. His only error had been in the way it would come about.

"It is a good contract, Tiana. And if you need any help in establishing yourself, I'll be glad to let some of our people work with you." After glancing down at the envelope, Bayne tossed it on the table.

"Thank you," she mumbled. "I'll get in touch with them."

Unsmilingly, he nodded before going to the door. His hand was on the knob when he turned to face her.

Tiana looked at him then, really looked for the first time. His eyes, usually so vividly expressive and yearningly alive, were glazed with a noble remoteness. Had it not been for the difference in color, they might have been twin mirrors of her own. And were those shadows around his eyes? Had time alone etched the crinkling lines a little deeper? She sighed. So much painting was taking its toll on her imagination.

"I didn't come here because of the letter. It was just an excuse." Bayne's hand dropped to his side. "I came to apologize to you."

Recalling the casual way in which Bayne had dismissed her sketches as straw men, Tiana could not keep the bloodless line of her mouth from compressing further. Did Bayne think she cared whether or not her work had been deemed worthy of a contract? Once she might have, but not now! "You said it yourself when you told me there was no accounting for the selections of some clients. It could just as easily have been someone else's drawings as mine so there is no need for an apology."

His brow furrowed, hooding his eyes. Bayne took a step towards her. "I wasn't talking about the sketches." His brow smoothed as his eyes searched hers. "I never meant to hurt you and I have reason to think I might have."

Startled, Tiana's eyes remained fastened to his.

Bayne smiled hesitantly. "You were right the very first day we met. I never should have judged you. Without realizing it, I measured you against the scale I had used for every other woman I had ever known. It was perhaps my biggest injustice because you are not like any other woman I have ever known."

Afraid to believe the words, fearful of trusting in the

sincerity of his voice, Tiana turned away. She could no longer believe in the kind of thing Bayne was saying. Tiana wrapped her arms around herself, her shoulders sagged as if she could keep his words from penetrating her heart.

"Peter returned today from Paris and I had a talk with him," Bayne stated softly.

"Oh!" Had it really been three weeks? "I had forgotten about him."

"Well, I didn't!" Bayne said. "I thought about Peter every minute of every day for three long weeks! I thought about him putting his arms around you, touching you and loving you. And I very quickly and quietly went insane."

"Insane?" Tiana's head jerked up.

"Yes," he whispered hoarsely from close behind her. "Won't you turn around and look at me, Tiana?"

"No!" She could not trust herself to look at him without revealing her feelings.

"Peter said you had a very transparent face. He also told me the right man could read his whole future in your eyes. Did he speak the truth?"

"I don't know what you mean," she said breathlessly. Had Peter broken his promise?

"Don't you?" There was a tacit amusement in the hush of his voice. "Well, according to Peter, every time you are with the man you love, a light glows within you, radiating through your entire expression. He said it is so pronounced that he was able to catch it on film. Do you think that's a fair evaluation?"

"I don't know," she breathed in a hesitant voice as a disabling weakness inched up the back of her legs. So this was to be Bayne's perfected torture! He had gotten the truth from Peter and now intended to deride her love for him; doubtlessly he would grind it under the heel of his cynicism.

"You know, Peter built a pretty good case for his theory. Fact is, he came right out and said that if I hadn't been at Look-Out-Point, he would have never gotten the picture for the campaign. He said . . ." There was an infinitesimal pause. ". . . you were in love with me. Is it true? Do you love me, Tiana?" An elemental tension was in the air and in his voice.

Even knowing Bayne would jeer at her admission, would insult her for her beliefs, Tiana could not bring herself to deny her love. To deny it would somehow tarnish it. She lifted her head high. "Yes."

Suddenly, Bayne's hands were on her shoulders, spinning her around. "Why didn't you let me know before?"

"So you could make fun of me? So you could call me a romantic idealist, a fool?" Anguish crept into her voice, blocking any other words. Her eyes were glued stubbornly to a point in space, refusing to focus on him.

"What have I done?" he enfolded her in his arms but her body was stiff as she fought the whirlpool of his virility. "Forgive me, Tiana?"

She threw back her head, her eyes frantically questioning him.

Green eyes welcomed brown. Without preparation, without thought, Tiana was lost in his eyes. It was a dreamlit paradise of unlimited scope and peace. It was her home. Rocked safely against the length of Bayne as he gathered her to him, Tiana knew it was real and right. His mouth covered hers and her soul became one with his.

"I love you, Tiana. It goes against the philosophy I adopted for myself, but so help me, I do love you." His voice was a husky whisper. "When I met you, I no longer believed in the abstract concept of love. I didn't want to believe in it. Yet from the moment I first saw you, I was drawn to you. You were so fresh and innocent, I could not believe you could survive untouched. Countless times I rationalized my feeling for you. I tried to convince myself that if I could just possess you, have an affair with you, I would get it out of my system. But it never seemed to work because I already loved you too much."

"I don't think I could have endured it, if you made love to me and then left me." Her eyes found the regret in his.

"I will spend the rest of my life making up for the shabby way I spoke to you. I love you beyond the measure of time itself. If it's any consolation to you, I could have never left you, especially if we had made love."

"But you said . . ."

"I know what I said! And I've been sorry ever since. I called you the next morning just as soon as the sun came up to apologize, but there was no answer. I tried to put you out of my mind, but by the time three weeks were up, I was ready to admit my love. I went to the airport with the intention of begging your forgiveness, but when Peter got off the plane without you, I almost went crazy."

"What happened?"

"Peter was as shocked as I was at your disappearance, Tiana. We caught a cab to your apartment and on the way over, he told me about your message and how he assumed you and I had patched things up. At the time, he was congratulating himself on a masterful feat of engineering."

"Oh no! You mean Peter planned the whole thing?" Tiana was on the glorious brink of laughter.

"He confessed it all; the bogus reason for taking you to Paris, his previous efforts to get us together, and the way he used your feelings for me to get his picture. If I hadn't been so concerned over your whereabouts

I probably would have taken him to task, right then. But there was no time for that because once we got to your place we had to figure out where you were. When Catherine found your suitcase in the closet, she guessed you came here. Which reminds me, I promised to telephone them if I found you." He planted a kiss on her nose.

One arm remained around her as he dialed the number and spoke a half dozen clipped words into the receiver. Tiana kept her head against his shoulder, knowing that whatever the future held for her, at this moment all her wishes and dreams had been fulfilled. As Bayne replaced the receiver, she lifted smiling eyes to him.

After kissing her, Bayne asked, "So, how soon can we have this wedding?"

"Wedding?" So happy, so at peace was Tiana that she had gone no further than Bayne's love.

He chuckled, "You certainly didn't think I could offer you less?"

"After what you . . ."

His lips swooped down to silence her. And when he raised his head, he said, "There is no past. There is only now and all the future. I can never make up for the jealousy, the insanity, that caused me to treat you so harshly. Will you ever forgive me?"

"I would be the last person to hold jealousy against you. I hated myself for being so jealous of Catherine. I thought for sure the two of you would get married," she admitted shyly.

"Let me explain about Catherine. She is a very dear and wonderful friend but contrary to popular opinion, we were never lovers. You see, I was once disappointed with love and I wanted no other involvements. Catherine for her own reasons felt the same way, so we combined forces in order to achieve business goals. For many years, it worked beautifully, until the day I met you."

Under the protective blanket of Bayne's love, Tiana laughingly confessed, "I never thought I had a chance. Catherine is so charming and sophisticated."

"She has nothing compared to what you hold for me. Tiana, you have something far more fundamental, more necessary for my life. You have a bewitching grace that has captured my heart and made it your slave. It is a special magic and when I hold you like this in my arms, it's like waltzing among the stars." Before Bayne's mouth met hers in passion's kiss, he paused to whisper along the curve of her lips. "Let me feel some of that magic of yours, Elf."

And with a little cry of joy, Tiana lifted her mouth to his.

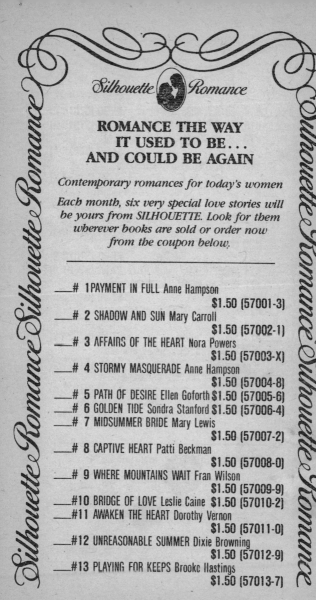

Silhouette ❦ *Romance*

ROMANCE THE WAY
IT USED TO BE...
AND COULD BE AGAIN

Contemporary romances for today's women

*Each month, six very special love stories will
be yours from SILHOUETTE. Look for them
wherever books are sold or order now
from the coupon below.*

___#14 RED, RED ROSE Tess Oliver $1.50 (57014-5)
___#15 SEA GYPSY Fern Michaels $1.50 (57015-3)
___#16 SECOND TOMORROW Anne Hampson
                                  $1.50 (57016-1)
___#17 TORMENTING FLAME Nancy John
                                  $1.50 (57017-X)
___#18 THE LION'S SHADOW Elizabeth Hunter
                                  $1.50 (57018-8)
___#19 THE HEART NEVER FORGETS Carolyn Thornton
                                  $1.50 (57019-6)
___#20 ISLAND DESTINY Paula Fulford
                                  $1.50 (57020-X)
___#21 SPRING FIRES Leigh Richards $1.50 (57021-8)
___#22 MEXICAN NIGHTS Jeanne Stephens
                                  $1.50 (57022-6)
___#23 BEWITCHING GRACE Paula Edwards
                                  $1.50 (57023-4)
___#24 SUMMER STORM Letitia Healy $1.50 (57024-2)
___#25 SHADOW OF LOVE Sondra Stanford
                                  $1.50 (57025-0)
___#26 INNOCENT FIRE Brooke Hastings
                                  $1.50 (57026-9)
___#27 THE DAWN STEALS SOFTLY Anne Hampson
                                  $1.50 (57027-7)

SILHOUETTE BOOKS, Department SB/1

1230 Avenue of the Americas, New York, N.Y. 10020

Please send me the books I have checked above. I am enclosing $_____
(please add 50¢ to cover postage and handling for each order, N.Y.S. and N.Y.C.
residents please add appropriate sales tax). Send check or money order—no
cash or C.O.D.s please. Allow up to six weeks for delivery.

NAME_____

ADDRESS_____

CITY_____ STATE/ZIP_____

SB/1-6/80